No More Chances

Also By Steven J. Conners

THE MADNESS OF POWER SERIES:
Book One: No More Chances
Book Two: A-B-C
Book Three: Heaven On Earth (coming in 2018)

NON-FICTION
A Voice of Reason

No More Chances

A Story of Eco-Terrorism

Book One: *The Madness of Power*

Steven J. Conners

STEVEN J. CONNERS / RENO, NV

Steven J. Conners
Reno, NV
www.stevenjconners.com

Publisher's Note: This is a work of fiction. Names, characters, places, and incidents are a product of the author's imagination. Locales and public names are sometimes used for atmospheric purposes. Any resemblance to actual people, living or dead, or to businesses, companies, events, institutions, or locales is completely coincidental.

No More Chances/ Steven J. Conners. -- 1st ed.
Print Edition ISBN 978-0-9991754-0-8
Kindle Edition ISBN 978-0-9991754-1-5

Dedicated to the young people of the world:

You must immediately stop the industrial pollution of your water, food and air and repair this worldwide catastrophe.

Only by fixing it will you and your children have a future.

Unfortunately, it is up to the X-Y-Z generations to tidy up the horrible mess which your predecessors have made.

—We are sincerely sorry.

Contents

Preface

Several years ago, my Granddaughter, Sabrina, and I watched a TV documentary, *The 11th Hour*, and two episodes of the Sundance Channel's *Big Ideas for A Small Planet*. As the credits rolled Sabrina, then a teenager, gave me a sermon on the way things were in the world and what needed to be done to make them better. She was full of ecological information and very passionate about her views.

That time with Sabrina inspired me to, again, attempt to finish this book about our many environmental problems. I pulled out a box stuffed with notes and research. The pages I had written were all neatly contained in a folder.

Most of the issues in this book have been on my mind for over forty years. That's a long time to hold onto ideas. When I started this book, I remembered reading somewhere that the best way to impart information was to use entertainment. Learning should be enjoyable. Even though this book is fiction, I hope the "action-adventure" is enough to both educate and entertain you.

In the early 1970s I read a book by Rachel Carson, *Silent Spring*, and saw two movies, *Day of the Dolphin* and *Soylent Green*, all of which greatly impressed me, and frightened me at the same time. These stories were grim. I read copies of *Mother Earth News*, got books on self-reliance, homemade energy, living underground, and became interested in the subjects of pollution and ecology. I read Al Gore's book, *An Inconvenient Truth*. Gore's book not only poses questions, but offers possible answers. It is quite shocking and well written.

It seemed that there was good reason to believe that the industrial paths humankind had chosen in the twentieth century could eventually lead to total human destruction. I recognized the unbelievable power and control that the corporate and government systems wielded over the environment, as well as the people of this country. These systems were in charge, but not doing a fair or equitable job.

True, we have newer and newer things for better living, but we've paid an extremely high price for these innovations. The air we breathe, the water we drink and the food we eat are all being polluted by these new technologies. Our rivers, streams and aquifers are filled with toxins. Our oceans are being poisoned and are dying. Sickness and death for progress and profits? By any measure, that is not a reasonable trade-off.

But how did we, as humans, allow this to happen?

I began to look for current information about these issues. What I found was astounding.

There is quite a lively "green movement" out there. Many excellent ideas, some of which are coming to fruition. This is a good thing. But is it too late? The ratio of "green" ideas that are being done to the continuation of "dirty" pollution is not even close to parity.

Humankind has always been at the mercy of nature. Nature is not predictable and it is a mighty force that must be reckoned with. History records that nature has caused humankind much pain and suffering. Lack of control over the elements motivated humans to attempt to dominate nature.

In the last few hundred years, humankind has learned to wield science and technology to overcome the great natural forces, damming and diverting rivers to increase crop production, finding ways to make it rain and curing most of the illnesses that plagued us for thousands of years.

It seems humankind's attempt to become God is no longer impossible.

But with great arrogance, he has overlooked the consequences of these actions. Through promiscuousness and selfish efforts, he has been adding his own mistakes to the ways of nature.

The results are horrendous and will eventually be fatal.

For nearly a century, scientific data has existed proving that using fossil fuel energy is a bad idea. Ultimately, the side effects outweigh the benefits. The resulting pollution is killing us.

Those who control the oil have made multi-trillions of dollars and continue to make those obscene profits today, exploiting the people and defying nature. Oil companies have always known that the pollution from gas and diesel engines, the toxins from the making of plastics and all oil-related products are deadly.

The awesome power of the United States government in partnership with major oil and chemical corporations, makes almost anything permissible. Greed facilitates manipulation of statistics, false assessments, and lying to the public.

Worldwide deforestation for wood products should be outlawed. We have gone too far. We forget that the function of the trees is to provide oxygen and clean the air of CO^2.

We, the USA, steadfastly refuse to acknowledge that we are causing and contributing to very dangerous global warming. Our government insists this is not true. That is a very unintelligent position to take. It makes us quite unpopular with the rest of the world. As of this writing, every nation in the world has approved the Kyoto Protocol and the Paris Agreement, except for the United States. How can that be?

I made some conclusions from these observations.

Of all the nations of the world, we are the biggest emitter of greenhouse gases, which cause global warming. The United States releases over 25% of the world's SO^4 gas. Methane, nitrous oxide and CFC's exist in quantities beyond acceptable per capita ratios. We are the most flagrant violators.

The governments and the corporations of the world are out of control, oblivious to the consequences of their actions. We seem to have a colossal impasse.

Ultimately, it may be nature itself, combined with modern technology that could save us from extinction.

This book, although a fiction based on very valid facts, offers other daring solutions. I am not suggesting that in real life, the violent and unlawful measures that my fictional characters employ are correct, or that they could, or should be copied or implemented. However… My hope is that readers may discover in these pages information they did not previously know, inspiring a new outlook and inspiring their own investigation. We are all individually responsible for the state of the environment in which we live.

The names and locations of the eco-violators referenced in these pages are, for the most part, fiction. But there is fact contained in this fiction. The real eco-violators know who they are and exactly what they're doing.

With that disclaimer made, I now promise that you will learn "what the dolphin has to say." Take heed of its warning.

Finally, I wish you to be entertained and informed.

Steven J. Conners
Vista, California
2017

One

Oil Company Protesters

It was a hot, humid San Francisco summer day. The swarm of lunch foot traffic ebbed and flowed around the plaza in front of the giant AP&G Oil building. Three men in dark suits pushed through the huge glass doors of the building, one after another, then stopped abruptly as a loud bullhorn blared from out of nowhere.

"Hey, you guys! You really love oil, right?"

The bullhorn voice seemed to come from directly above the three men. Each looked up at the doorway searching for the source of the voice.

"Do it now! Wear some of it, you crummy capitalist pigs."

Four large buckets of crude oil were thrown from opposite sides of the doorway of the AP&G Oil Company office building directly onto the three executives.

The man speaking on the bullhorn mockingly yelled, "Ka-ching! Ka-ching! Ka-ching!"

The three executives were covered from head to toe in the black-brown goop. It burned their eyes. They lost their balance and slipped, falling into the pooled oil on the pavement.

To see dignity reduced to comic proportions was funny. The crowd of protestors laughed loudly. It was only human.

Eric Atkins laughed, too. He was a recent participant in the activist group known as CAOP (Citizens Against Oil Pollution). It was on the streets of San Francisco that he had heard about the CAOP activists and went to one of their meetings.

The CAOP were much like many activist groups of the 70s. Not very informed, or well organized, but very vocal. They were against the pollution created everywhere by big oil. The only thing Eric knew was that this group was anti-big oil. The CAOP message had appealed to Eric. He believed that being part of the group might offer some fun with decent kids trying to make a positive difference in the world. And, there were so many really cute girls.

But this violent act stunned him.

At first, Eric was frozen in place as the protesters dispersed very rapidly. They ran away. These young activists didn't want to be caught and arrested by the police.

Eric had a sudden fit of empathy and downright guilt. He ran over to the executives who had fallen to the ground. They were moaning and dazed.

As Eric took his T-shirt off and knelt down, he spoke in a solid but soothing commanding voice. "Keep your eyes closed." Quickly, he blotted the eyes of each man and continued. "Just sit calmly where you are with your eyes closed. I'm going to get some help. I'll be right back."

Eric went inside the building and got the security guard to call the fire department, ambulances and the police. The fire department would know how to "de-oil" them and the men would undoubtedly need some medical attention.

Eric had completely forgotten that he was part of the CAOP group. Now, he was merely doing what he thought should be done to help these unfortunate victims.

Upon returning to the three oil-soaked men, one of them identified himself as Elvin Carter, a vice president at AP&G Oil Company. He sincerely thanked Eric for his help and, with grimy hands, the man retrieved a business card from his coat pocket and asked Eric to be in touch with him.

Eric nodded and then heard the sirens. He decided it was time for him to leave the scene. He didn't want to get caught up with the police, either. He stuck the card in his pocket and quickly ducked around the corner.

It was a hot summer day and many people were shirtless. The loss of his olive-drab T-shirt was no problem.

As Eric walked he thought, "Maybe the CAOP activist group is too much. Throwing crude oil on guys was just mean and not very effective. It's okay to protest, but they went too far. Whatever the CAOP complaints might be, a more peaceful and sensible approach would be better. I'm not going to any more of their meetings. They're nuts."

In a few days, Eric took out the oil-stained business card and called Elvin Carter for an appointment. The secretary to Mr. Carter was expecting Eric's call. The meeting was scheduled for the next day at 2:00 p.m.

Eric walked into the Atlantic Pacific & Gulf Oil Company office building. The architecture was very extravagant; obviously meant to impress the onlooker with the wealth of AP&G Oil.

The directory showed Mr. Carter's office was on the fourteenth floor. He had the entire top floor.

As Eric stepped off the elevator he was again met with the impression of enormous wealth.

A reception person took Eric to Mr. Carter's office.

Elvin Carter was a medium-sized man who looked every bit the executive in his dark blue suit. He got up from his desk and put out his hand to Eric. "I'm Elvin Carter and you're Eric Atkins, my hero. Well, I thank you, again, young man. The doctors at the hospital told me that if you hadn't blotted away that oil with your T-shirt and told us to keep our eyes shut, we could have gone blind. You saved us. By the way, that T-shirt had USMC on it. Are you a Marine?

"I was, sir. 'Nam for three years, and two months. Wounded once. Got out alive."

"I'm ex-Marine, too. Korea. *Semper Fi.*"

"*Semper Fi.*"

"Eric, do you have any idea who did this to us?"

Eric lied. "No, sir. I was just listening to their rant and suddenly they threw the oil at you guys." Eric was very glad he didn't sign anything and didn't go back to any of the CAOP meetings.

"What are your plans, Eric?"

"Going to UC Berkeley this fall to hopefully get a Masters in Marine Biology."

"That's great. I've got a little check for you. Thought you could use it. Students are always short of cash. I want you to keep in touch with me, Eric. When you get that Master's certificate you come and see me. There'll be a job for you here at AP&G Oil."

Eric was overwhelmed. "Thank you, Mr. Carter, but you don't have to…"

"Nonsense. It's my pleasure to help a fine boy like you."

The check from Mr. Carter was for one thousand dollars. Eric was thankful for that check. It gave him some back-up for school expenses.

Eric Atkins had joined the Marines the summer he got out of high school. He was in Vietnam for three hard years of unbearable jungle conditions, and terrible killing.

When the war was over, he mustered out of the service and used his GI bill to go to University of California at Irvine to get his BA degree.

This past spring he graduated from UCI and was now in San Francisco for the summer. He was just going to kick around a bit, before he started his Master's courses in advanced Marine Biology and Ocean Engineering at UC Berkeley.

Now it was the middle of June and Eric decided that even with this windfall he ought to get a job. School was coming in two months and he needed a steady flow of cash. He hoped to find some work connected with biology or oceans.

He walked the streets in the Haight-Ashbury district looking at all the kiosks. He spied a job listing on a Berkeley bulletin board.

LAB ASSISTANT WANTED: Biology background. Full time student. Hours to fit your schedule. Call Prof. Altman.

This job sounded perfect. Eric pulled one of the little tabs from the poster and decided to call Professor Altman immediately for an appointment. He walked over to a pay phone and dialed the number printed on the back of the tab.

Altman himself answered the phone. After a brief chat Eric was told to come to the Professor's office at 4:00 p.m. that very afternoon.

Eric was excited and took a shortcut through the science building and stopped when he spied a beautiful girl manning a table for the Sierra Club.

He noticed a stack of brochures on a table. *Join the Sierra Club!* He picked up a brochure and began to read about the history of the organization.

Casually looking at the name badge of the girl behind the table, he asked with a sincere, but flirtatious smile. "So, tell me about the Sierra Club, uh, Elaine."

She smiled back at him and answered his question by reciting the information on the back of the brochure.

In May 1892, John Muir and a group of professors from the University of California at Berkeley and Stanford University founded an association intended to protect and preserve the Sierra Nevada. The Sierra Club has grown into one of the largest conservation organizations in the world, lending its resources to agriculture, biotechnology, energy, forests, wilderness, oceans, pollution, waste management, urban land use, water resources, wildlife conservation and population growth. There are currently over 700,000 members.

"Okay. Very nicely recited." Eric said. "All stuff I'm interested in, neatly available in one club. I'll join, but only if you'll have some coffee and a little conversation with me when you're done."

Elaine ignored his come-on and filled out the application form asking him a few questions about his age and address and then pushed the form toward Eric for him to sign.

He paid her the fee and Elaine gave him his receipt. On the back of the receipt was her answer. "I'm off at 4:30. See you at *The Samich Joint,* just across from the record shop."

Eric put the receipt and the brochure in his pocket. With his joining of the Sierra Club, a date with a beautiful girl, an appointment for a job with Professor Altman, he was on cloud nine, and went happily on his way.

It was 4:00 p.m. on the button. Eric was on time. He knocked on Professor Altman's door and a gruff voice said, "Come!"

Inside the tiny little office, sitting at a very cluttered desk was Professor Howard Altman. In his late sixties, Eric thought, and the professor needed a shave and a haircut.

"So you want to learn about marine biology, do you? Well, it's a tedious and sometimes discouraging job that never ends. When you find out one thing, then you are compelled to look for another. Tell me why you are interested in marine biology, young man."

Eric hadn't expected to be put on the grill this quick. Altman was direct and Eric was a little timid in his answer. "Well, since high school, I've always been interested in biology. Guess it was my teacher, Professor Vance. He wrote our textbook and was writing another. Working with students, he said, gave him insight for his writing. I had Professor Vance for Biology I and II. He was inspirational, brilliant, exciting and thorough. My interest in the oceans seemed like a logical progression. We know very little..."

"B. B. Vance, is one of my dearest friends. We went to the same school and shared the same dorm. A great guy, a fine scientist and good teacher. You had Vance for biology both years in high school, did you? Well, he's the best spiritual influence you could get. You've got the job, young man. Be warned, I'll expect you to live up to B.B.'s standards, you know. I'll see you here tomorrow at 9:00 a.m. sharp."

It was all falling into place. The school, the job and the girl. This was a magic time.

Eric arrived at *The Samich Joint* a little early. He found an outside table and began to read a book.

Elaine, came walking up. She stood for a moment, so Eric could see all of her, then turned and plopped down in a chair. "I know it's not hard work, but I'm really tired, and hungry, too. Whatcha gonna have, good lookin'?"

Eric was happy. Nobody ever called him good looking to his face. He knew he was handsome, but this was really sexy. A girl coming on to him. He liked it.

"Well, I don't know the menu at this place."

Elaine suggested. "I do. Have you ever had a Tube-Burger? It's a long rolled burger in a big whole-wheat hotdog bun, with everything on the top. Tomatoes, cucumbers, pickles, peppers. It's like a full lunch, and it's really good."

"Yeah, I'll try it. One for you, too. My treat."

He put in the order and returned to the table. Pointing at the name tag on her blouse he said. "By the way, if that's Elaine..." Eric hesitated. He decided not to do the old gag about 'what did you name the other one?' "...I mean what's your last name?"

"Elaine Rebecca Kroslin. And, you are Eric Atkins. You're not."

"Not?"

"Not Jewish."

"Yeah, I'm not Jewish, or Christian, or Buddhist, or Muslim, or anything. Don't know where I came from, don't know why I'm here and don't know where I'll go when I die."

"You're religious, though. You belong to the church of 'I don't know.' That's good, because I think that way, too."

"So... You're Jewish?"

"Born Jewish, but I'm a practicing "don't knower.""

To his amazement, Eric fell immediately in love with this bright, beautiful, sexy girl. He knew he wanted to marry Elaine right away.

Eric saw a small poster on a kiosk. One of his hero's, Roger Revelle was going to speak at Berkeley. Dr. Revelle was one of the living legends of socio-environmentalism and oceanography. He was definitely going to that lecture.

Roger Revelle had been a director of the Scripps Institute of Oceanography and was instrumental in founding the University of California at San Diego. He was a very inspirational and learned man. Revelle was taking time away from his current position as founder and director of the Harvard Center for Population and Development Studies to speak at the University at Berkeley, which was his alma mater.

Eric sat in the large auditorium with a little notebook. Eric did not want to depend on his memory to capture the information and wisdom he knew Dr. Revelle would share.

During the lecture, Eric noted Revelle's statements about the general increase in worldwide air and water temperatures. Revelle called it "global warming." Dr. Revelle described the worldwide burning of fossil fuels and industrial emissions as causes for the excessive release of carbon dioxide into the atmosphere, and cited this as the main source of this "global warming."

Eric quickly scribbled snippets of what Revelle was telling them:

A graduate school is a place where professors make colleagues of their students.

One characteristic of a research-oriented graduate school should be that it does not have too rigid a program or too well thought out a plan...What we need if we're going to emphasize research, is to make things messier and more chaotic.

Eric could barely write fast enough.

The scientific study of the earth as a whole is becoming ever more dependent on an increased understanding of that part of the earth which is covered by sea water. Our definition of oceanography is thus gradually broadening to be simply: The science that is done at sea. We know more about the surface of the moon than about the topography of the seafloor.

Inspired, Eric silently vowed to try to find a way to work toward stopping the pollution of the land and oceans.

Two years later, after receiving his master's degree in marine biology, Eric decided to ask Elvin Carter at AP&G Oil Company for the job he'd offered to Eric.

AP&G Oil was one of the largest crude oil producers and refiners in the world. They had a huge refinery and storage facilities in Texas and refinery and petrochemical operations in the Los Angeles area. Their off-shore drilling rigs were dotted all over the shores of California and the Gulf of Mexico. AP&G Oil Company had a main office located in San Francisco and other offices in Houston and New York.

Elvin Carter, a first vice president at AP&G Oil, was a man of his word. He immediately hired Eric to start work in their Oceanic Environmental Studies division.

Eric was thrilled beyond words. Now he could make a difference and help to clean up the oceans.

His new job consisted of observation and research. He assisted in the conducting of controlled experiments regarding ocean oil spills. His background in biology helped him explore the effects of these spills on animals and plants. Sometimes Eric was out to sea or on the shoreline and at other times he was in the laboratory. He loved his job. All questions. Few answers.

Soon, his engagement to Elaine finally came to fruition and they set a date to be married.

The wedding was a private affair with just a few of their close friends invited to attend. A justice of the peace officiated at the ceremony and the reception was held at *The Samich Joint.*

Elaine and Eric decided to postpone their honeymoon, but agreed they would take that festive trip within the year.

Eric's bachelor days had ended. He moved into Elaine's apartment, because she had furniture. He had very little and his move was done easily with two bags and two boxes.

Their home was a small place, but they were happy to be with each other. They looked forward to building a long marriage together.

Marine biologists are not in great demand. Eric was thankful for his job at AP&G Oil Company.

Elaine had graduated with a masters degree in education and began teaching elementary school in San Francisco.

Their life was enjoyable. They lived well and saved lots of money.

Elaine wanted to have children.

Soon she was pregnant and they were both very excited.

But, in her third month, Elaine had a miscarriage. The baby was slightly deformed and the doctor requested a thorough physical to be done on Eric.

The results came back from the lab. It was the doctor's opinion that Eric and Elaine were quite healthy and normal. The doctor told them that these things sometimes happen and they should try again as soon as possible.

In a few months Elaine was pregnant, but again she miscarried during her first trimester.

Elaine decided that they should wait for a long time before trying to have children again.

The real cause of her miscarriages would not be known for many years.

Two

Working for the Man

Eric had been working at AP&G Oil for nearly a year. Because of his background and a recommendation from Elvin Carter, Eric was allowed to create his own projects.

His first idea was to correlate all of the spill incidents involving AP&G Oil and see if there was a pattern.

He soon learned that the analyses of the oil accidents were all based on money. The losses were assessed, not by toxic damage to the environment, but merely in dollar losses to the company.

When Eric tried to gather and correlate non-financial data on these 'accidents' he inevitably ran into dead ends. Most of the relevant files were kept in four heavy locked filing cabinets marked "Classified" and were not available to Eric without authorization. Many times, Eric requested permission to use these files in order to complete his studies accurately. He was always denied access.

Frustrated, Eric went to Elvin Carter to make a new request for permission to use these files.

Carter smiled. "Now, now, Eric, you must be patient and follow the directions of your superiors. Why do you want to get into those files, anyway?"

Eric stammered and answered, "Well, uh, because all of the available information presented so far are just summaries. I want the details, the facts, all of the data involved with the spills into the oceans. This is what you hired me to do, Mr. Carter."

Carter replied, "All right. Let's say you have access to all of the information. What will you do with it?"

"Correlate that information to show the impact, not just in terms of dollars, and make forecasts."

Carter was getting peeved. "Eric, please understand, as each of those unfortunate accidents happened we took extreme measures to successfully clean up the spills. Those cases are closed. Our job has been done."

"I know this, but by gathering and analyzing all of the data related to the accidents I might be able to design systems for the prevention of spills."

"I cannot go against company protocols just for you. I must deny you access to those files. That is final."

"But why does that information have to stay hidden? What's so secret? Why are the files classified?"

"I won't answer that. Now, please go back to your office, Eric. I order you to stop this project of yours. You'll do the work assigned to you, now. No more side projects. This matter is closed."

Eric left Elvin Carter and slunk down the hall. He had been reprimanded. Although he was a little depressed, he was slowly morphing that into a growing determination.

The meeting with Carter was very bad. Eric did not like being talked to in that way. The fact that he was now officially limited in his work made him more obsessed with looking at those files. What was in those cabinets that Elvin Carter did not want him to see? What damning information was hidden away and hopefully forgotten? He had to know.

Eric stopped at the file room on the way back to his office. There were four big filing cabinets, each with a vertical iron bar running through the handles of the drawers. A lock on top prevented the opening of each cabinet. Casually, Eric looked to see if the cabinets were hooked up to a security system. There were no contact plates and no wires to be seen. He looked at the heavy locks. Key locks. He wrote down the serial numbers and the makes of the locks.

After work Eric went to the library and got books on locks. He found a description of the very locks on the cabinets. Then he studied a couple of books about opening locks and how to make lock picks. He made copious notes. All he needed, now, was the right time.

Christmas day provided the perfect opportunity. No one would be in the offices. If he were seen, there would be no problem. Eric was allowed to come and go as he pleased.

Early in the morning he began his burglary. He was amazed at how easy it was to open the locks. The drawers were simply marked on the outside in alphabetical order. He began with the 'A' drawer. Inside he found a divider titled: "Spills and Leaching." The files going from front to back were in date order, most recent to oldest. He pulled the records and briskly walked to the copy room and began to photocopy everything in each file.

"No time to read. Can do that at home. Just copy all of them," he said out loud to himself.

The next drawer contained the legal information relevant to the first drawer. Files were tagged by name and date—individual lawsuits, class action lawsuits, citations from the EPA and OSHA—all the damning information and histories of malfeasance by AP&G Oil. From these files Eric copied only the summary pages. The hefty remainder in each drawer contained the depositions and transcripts of the proceedings and went on for hundreds of pages. All he wanted were the allegations and final judgments.

Eric was done before noon. Copying the files did not take as long as he expected and surprisingly, they all fit neatly into his large attaché case.

Eric boldly walked past the security guard, wishing him a "Merry Christmas," and left the building with no trouble.

Elated, he gleefully thought, "My God. I've become a thief. And, I'm pretty good at it!"

Back home, Eric took the attaché case containing the files to the room he called his office. He wanted to open it and look at the files, but he put the case in the corner of the room and patiently decided to wait until later. He wanted to enjoy what was left of this Christmas Day with Elaine.

That night, with Elaine fast asleep, Eric went to his home office room and opened his attaché case.

First, he separated the papers into three piles. The reports of the spills and leaching, the complaints as filed and the decisions made on each case.

Then he took a blank piece of paper from his desk and drew two lines down the length of the page. He labeled each column: ALLEGED, then REAL, and the last VERDICT. This would allow him to see a synopsis of each incident at a glance. After filling in the columns on his overview page he started another page and kept on reading, quickly scanning each case.

Eric sorted and paper-clipped the pages and put them in new manila folders. This process occupied him all night. He finished just as the sun was coming up.

The picture had become frighteningly clear. The allegations in the lawsuits were correct. The AP&G records admitted and corroborated those charges. But the outcome of each legal action indicated that complicity between AP&G Oil and the EPA certainly existed. In the court decisions, AP&G Oil was never ordered to correct the cause of the pollution. They were only required to do superficial clean-up and pay a fine. After some time, violation citations were issued by the EPA for non-payment, but they were never enforced and very little cash was paid out by AP&G Oil.

Conclusion: Big Oil-Big Chemical and the EPA appeared to be in bed with each other.

Eric was happy with the Sierra Club, but he decided to join another activist organization. It was called *Greenpeace*.

Although officially founded in the sixties as the *Don't Make a Wave* movement to stop nuclear testing in Alaska, about 1970 it changed its name to *Greenpeace*. This organization was devoted to making the public aware of the damage that was being done to the environment by rampant pollution. It used, as its platform, passive resistance and publicity.

Greenpeace was always on the lookout for someone with new information who would speak out under their banner. It seemed to Eric that *Greenpeace* could offer the perfect forum to tell the public about the information he had discovered at AP&G Oil.

A few days after joining, Eric received a call, in response to his request, from the *Greenpeace* director asking him to speak at their meeting on Sunday afternoon. It was Tuesday. It gave him little time to prepare, but he accepted the invitation and went to work on the writing.

In constructing his speech, he had to be careful to avoid naming AP&G Oil and the particulars of the purloined information from their files, as well as his conclusions. Yet, with an innate sense of integrity, he was compelled to be truthful. Eric wrote a first draft of his speech and then went back and lined out or used other words for the final version.

Sunday arrived. He was there and prepared and after a flowery introduction, he began. "Hello. My name is Eric Atkins and what I am about to tell you will not only inform you, but surprise you, as well. For years we all have suspected that the EPA is an ineffective branch of government. A lot of noise, but with little effect. Their efforts are not genuine. They're a ruse. Oh, they hand out citations to the offending corporations, but after careful research in several cases, it's clear that their actions are nothing but a slap on the wrist and nothing changes. The oil spills in the oceans, the oil and chemical spills on land and the pollution and leaching into the lakes and aquifers and ground water are the stuff of nightmares. Millions and millions of people's health and their very lives are affected now, but also, their futures, as well. Children born deformed, miscarriages, lung, bladder, liver and kidney cancers happening more frequently, all because these big corporations won't stop the careless production and handling of their oil and chemicals. These oil corporations are making vast amounts of money at the cost of maiming and killing people, animals and the environment.

"As these big corporations and their polluting ways go on. I'm sorry to say that they, and the EPA, are quite oblivious and unfeeling to the harm that they are causing. The Environmental Protection Agency, the government's watchdog and policeman, the guardian of the people, is not doing its job. Is it lack of concern? Indifference? Apathy? All of that, but really it's just greed! The glorious EPA doesn't stop these polluters. After all, the big oil corporations pay huge taxes and contribute immense dollars to federal, state and local government political campaigns. They even have been accused of electing the president. They are wealthy and powerful.

"And, how do I know all of this? Well I work for one of these great polluters and I have seen the evidence of their crimes. It became clear to me that big oil and big government are one in the same. Yes, we crusade. We petition. We write letters. We meet and talk. We make the public aware. Yet, we get no results. The pollution continues with no end in sight. So, what are we to do? Well, at this time, I'm not prepared to make specific suggestions, but I assure you, that something drastic must be done. I leave you to decide whether you and your families will continue to be poisoned in the name of corporate profits. If they can't, or won't hear us, then they must feel us. *Acta Non Verba*. Actions, not words! I thank you for listening, and good luck to us all!"

The small group sincerely applauded. He hoped he'd impressed upon them the seriousness of the situation.

Elaine was very proud of Eric, but her intuition caused her to be very worried for him. Even though he was right, he might have gone too far. Said too much.

After the holidays, Eric returned to work. On his desk was a note asking him to come to Elvin Carter's office.

Carter said, "Well, I hope you had wonderful holidays. Hopefully, this will be a bright New Year for us all."

"Thank you, sir." Eric steeled himself as Carter motioned for him to sit in the chair in front of Carter's desk.

"You're a member of *Greenpeace*, are you not?" Carter paced around Eric.

Eric nodded.

"Yes, yes, so I've been told. Well, that little speech you gave on Sunday was quite inspirational. It was videotaped. I've read the transcription. You're a firebrand, Eric. Do you know how much in conflict with AP&G policy you are?"

"Yes I do Mr. Carter, and I have spoken to you many times about these things. You must do something...

"...I must do something?" Carter raised his voice. "Who the hell are you to tell me how to do my job? Who are you to preach ethics to me, or anyone else? I believed in you, Eric; trusted you. I had faith in you. You are talented, but you are misguided."

Carter wheeled around and bent over Eric's chair, looking him straight in the eye. "Eric, our classified files have been broken into. Know anything about that?"

Eric didn't flinch.

Carter stood up straight and took up his place behind his giant oak and leather desk. "No, no. I didn't think you would. Well, many a good man has been hanged for something he did not do. And I'm about to hang you."

Carter seated himself and placed both arms on the desk leaning forward toward Eric. "You're a radical, Eric. You are finished in the petrochemical industry. I will send out the word to other corporations. You have been blackballed, boy. Now, without further comment, Eric Atkins you are discharged immediately from the AP&G Oil Company."

Eric stood up and turned to leave.

"And, don't go back to your office. Your personal things are being boxed up. You can retrieve them at the security station in the lobby. And wait..."

Eric turned back.

"Here is your generous, if I might say so, severance check. Good bye, Eric."

Eric took the check and that was that.

Three

The Honeymoon

In 1977 Paul Watson, who had been the skipper on several *Greenpeace* sailing expeditions, became adversarial toward *Greenpeace*. They didn't agree on strategies. He publicly spoke out against the lack of aggressive intervention and the pacifist philosophy of *Greenpeace*.

Watson was expelled from *Greenpeace* for his comments and very quickly formed his own organization, calling it *Sea Shepherd Conservation Society*.

Now Captain Watson, he began a vigorous campaign of direct action to ram, damage or sink, commercial whaling ships in violation of international laws. Part of his mission statement included: "…using innovative direct-action tactics to investigate, document, and take action when necessary to expose and confront illegal activities on the high seas."

As Eric read of Watson's exploits he came to agree with his philosophy and strategy. He wanted to join him.

Most of the voyages lasted just a few weeks. Each of the crew members were required to complete the mission, but they could leave anytime when the ship came to port.

Eric resigned from *Greenpeace* and embarked on an expedition with Paul Watson aboard *The Sea Shepherd*.

This single trip affirmed for Eric the principal of actions, not words. Captain Paul Watson became the newest hero in Eric's pantheon of great human beings.

During Eric's absence, Elaine continued to teach school. It kept her busy and allowed their cash flow to continue.

Elaine had undying faith in her husband. She knew that soon he was going to do something incredibly big.

Eric's experiences with the Sierra Club, *Greenpeace* and now the excursion on *The Sea Shepherd*, were enough to teach Eric that the environment needed some real help. Mankind must stop polluting his world. But, how to stop him? Eric knew he needed to do his part in aiding these organizations. Back from the voyage with Captain Watson, he needed some peace and quiet to think and sort out just how he was going to do this.

Elaine came to the rescue. Time for their honeymoon.

It was spring break and the perfect time for them to travel. They decided to go down the coast to La Jolla for their long awaited celebratory trip.

Eric needed to figure out what his next move might be, and he could visit the Scripps Institute of Oceanography. They could just relax, kick back for a while on the La Jolla beach and explore the area together.

Tired of the long drive from San Francisco, they stopped in Malibu.

As they were checking in to a hotel, Eric heard Dr. John Lilly's name mentioned in a conversation somewhere in the lobby. Eric asked the desk clerk. "Does John Lilly live nearby?"

The clerk answered. "Yes, he has a house by the beach."

Eric had read about the remarkable John Cunningham Lilly. He was a pioneer of interspecies communication. Lilly claimed he was able to talk with dolphins. He also was an oceanic and environmental activist. Eric was determined to meet this amazing and talented man.

Their bags in the room, Eric told Elaine that he had something he must do and he would be back shortly.

He rented a car and drove over the zigzagging mountain roads to John Lilly's house at Zuma Beach.

Upon arrival, even though they had never met, Dr. Lilly welcomed Eric to his home like a long-lost son. Over glasses of wine, they talked and talked. Dr. John Lilly became deeply interested in Eric's future.

"Please call me John, Eric. I warn you now of the futility and inherent danger of being an activist. Everyone will think you're a nutcase, and in the end nothing much will be accomplished. If you want to do something, a low profile is much better. Keep your plans secret."

A light bulb went on in Eric's mind. "Keep a low profile. It worked for Bruce Wayne and Batman. Why not?"

Lilly urged Eric to get his doctorate. He told him that without a doctorate he would not be taken seriously.

Eric asked Dr. Lilly about the movie *Day of the Dolphin*.

"I've seen that film, and I acknowledge that some of it was factual, although it was 'Hollywood-ed' up a bit."

"Dr. Lilly, er, John, I want to ask you about a scene that is stuck in my mind. It was the one with George Scott standing in the water, talking with a dolphin. If I may ask, what do you think the dolphin said?"

"Well, you're inviting me to do some creative writing, Eric. Here's what I think the dolphin might have said." John Lilly scribbled a few words on a piece of paper and handed the paper to Eric.

Eric read the note and smiled. "John, I will keep this and always remember what it means. I'm sure this is exactly what the dolphin said."

That meeting was the beginning of a life-long friendship. At the end of the day, Dr. John C. Lilly became another man who would influence and shape Eric's destiny.

As suggested by Dr. Lilly, Eric enrolled in Hardeston Institute of Marine Biology and in less than two years he graduated, *cum laude*, with doctorates in marine biology and ocean management. After graduation

Eric was invited by Dean Davis to join the faculty at Hardeston as assistant professor of marine biology to Professor George Rossey.

Within Eric's first year Professor Rossey died, leaving the marine biology department without anyone in charge

Eric requested the job and immediately was given the position as head of the department.

Eric remembered John Lilly's advice and kept a low profile. Yet, in teaching, the activist in him kept coming out. He voiced his ideas, sometimes, a little too much.

Four

Hardeston Institute of Marine Biology

The marine biology building was very old. The interior of this lecture hall was quite offensive. The lingering chemicals made it smell musty and quite malodorous. A randomly placed, slightly swinging shade light over the teacher's table and the dirty hanging fluorescent lights, with their muted dim yellow glow, gave this aged teaching lecture hall/lab an incredibly gloomy and dingy atmosphere.

Over the years, thousands of young men and women had used the dark slate-topped tables and the wooden desk seats and learned much about the mysteries of life that were hidden in the world of biology.

Not so long ago, Eric Atkins had been a student here himself, committing to environmental science as his lifetime endeavor. For years now he'd taught at Hardeston University. He was a full professor of Marine Biology and Ocean Management. Teaching about the condition of the world's seas and ecology was his profession, but environmental protection and repair were still his passions.

On this particular day, half of the seats were filled in the lecture hall. A few of the students were paying attention. Some of them were sleeping or daydreaming as Professor Atkins droned on and on.

Eric was thinking of other things as he automatically spoke, giving the students more and more boring facts. "The twelve most dangerous toxins, the ones that are in our food and water and air, are sometimes referred to as the 'Dirty Dozen.' They are, as follows: aldrin, chlordane, dieldrin, endrin, heptachlor, hexachlorobenzene…"

The students shifted in their seats as Eric droned on, "…mirex, toxaphene…"

Eric's face was blank. "…polychlorinated biphenyls, polychlorinated dibenzo-p-dioxins, polychlorinated dibenzofurans, DDT." He summarized as if reading from a textbook. "These chemicals are used in, and/or are the byproducts of many industries. The resulting un-managed pollution is slowly killing all of us."

After years of teaching at Hardeston University Eric was frustrated and bored with this job. He continued to mumble and mutter on. "I want you to look up each of these chemicals and give me a paragraph of definition and description, including what effects you think each one of these chemicals might be having on all life forms."

The students collectively groaned.

Eric was not completely unfazed. He thought, "What's going on here? These are vital subjects. Don't these kids understand that I'm talking about their future? The future of mankind! And why can't they concentrate on this stuff? What's more important than these issues? Music? Dating? Fashion? Movies? TV?"

His silent resentment grew. "Are they blasé, or brain-dead, or am I just a bad teacher? Am I boring them with too many details? Damn it all. I'm trying. But, hell, this stuff really is dry."

As his inward focus shifted, he spoke aloud to the students. "So, you see, these chemicals are quite different from… Ah, this is all HORSE SHIT!" he said loudly.

The students were stunned into paying attention.

"This isn't the important information. You got most of this in high school biology. I want you to know the facts. The dangers. The consequences. The real deal. The big picture."

Some of them were paying attention now.

Eric stopped abruptly, and raised his voice to a shout. "GOD DAM-NIT! You over there, wake that guy up. Now listen, you've got to understand the real hazards. I've said this before, and I'm going to say it again: the ecology of the world is the most important issue that you will encounter in your lifetimes. If we don't stop those greedy corporations from polluting our air, our water and our food chain, we will all eventually die from these horrible conditions and the human race will cease to exist. This is important, people!"

He had their attention now. The class fell silent as Eric remembered the last time he was reprimanded, and his promise to Dean Arthur R. Davis: "Dean Davis, I will only teach biology and will never criticize the oil and chemical companies in any way."

He thought. "So, I made him that promise. So what?"

Eric's passion was showing again. He had the kids interested and was primed to go even further. He knew he was in very deep water, but he was on a roll and really didn't care.

Eric leaned across his marble topped lab desk. "Somehow, I don't think I'm getting through to you. You're not in here to learn how to get along with the pollution. You're here to learn how to stop it; how to clean up what has been done. And most importantly, how to prevent it from happening again. If this concept doesn't excite you, you shouldn't be here. If it does get your interest, you should be asking me the hard questions and not hoping to hear pleasant answers. Mankind has serious problems and you have to solve them!"

Eric walked from in back of his desk moving toward the front lab tables. He tried to look each student in the room square in the eye. "Now let's go around the room and hear from you. I want to know where your heads are, what your observations and proposals might be. I want to hear new ideas that could fix this worldwide ecological mess. I want you to seriously consider the problem."

Eric pointed. "You, down here in the front. What do you think can and should be done to correct some of these troubles with our environment?"

A young man, with a smug attitude spoke out. "Well, you've got some of us pegged, doc. Some of us are just killing time in this class. I see your point, though. But in a way, this is such a big problem that I, for one, consider that pollution can never be eliminated. Sure, we have to learn to modify what we're doing and then hope for the best. I see my future as an ecological maintenance man."

Some students giggled. Eric didn't think it was funny.

"A maintenance man. Hell, you don't need a degree for that job, boy, just a broom and trash can. You shouldn't be in here, you should be working on a garbage truck."

The entire class laughed as Eric picked another person. "How about you, Ms. Budwick. Maintenance? Reconstruction? Cessation?"

"Well, Professor Atkins, I think the challenge here is to find out how to cure the current problems of pollution and then to create methods to prevent that pollution from happening again. So, all of the above. It's a job of re-education and reconstruction, and of course, cessation."

Eric was delighted.

"At last, someone with a brain who actually USES it! Now the rest of you, jump in. What's the most important thing we can do now?" Eric selected a raised hand in the back.

"Professor. Professor. Thank you. I've been to every one of your classes this year. Never missed one. I've gotta say, though, I've listened to some of the driest facts ever uttered in any class, here. Professor, you state the questions, but you never get to the core of the problem, just the academic biology crap. I mean, okay, we will all start tomorrow to clean up the world. But how do we fight the pollution and the polluters at the same time? Like, I mean, it's the big corporations who have made the mess. Can't the EPA stop them? Wow. I guess that's influencing policy and politics. Maybe politics is what I should be learning."

"God help you if you do. You do my heart good, young man. You have paid attention and you have the problem properly analyzed. Well, the EPA can't, or won't, stop them. They sue them and the suits stay in the courts for years and then the corporate offender just pays a fine. And during all those years in court, the corporation goes on polluting. The EPA is ineffectual because they do nothing to stop pollution. They just collect fines from the corporations. Those corporations have realized that it is millions of dollars cheaper to pay the EPA fines than to clean up the pollution or modify their production methods."

Eric smiled. "You know, I apologize for being boring. I think we'll put a hold on some of that dry science, as you called it, and try a little social science as it applies to the ecological pollution problem. I can tell you that political power and greed are at the base of it all. So, think twice about being a politician. Now, let's see how this all works."

Eric went to the blackboard and wrote the word "CITATION" and under that the word "methyl chloride," then turned and faced the class. "Let's take a look at an EPA citation. Say it's the United States vs. Big Chemical Corporation. The EPA has alleged that Big Chem has for many years been negligent in its disposal of methyl chloride and that the EPA, and outside experts, have warned Big Chem that it has very severe methyl chloride run-off that is polluting the aquifer in and around their plant in Burgs-burg. Big Chem responds and says it has the problem under advisement. EPA says Big Chem must cease the pollution condition and clean-up the mess. Big Chem says they have the problem in full discussion and will present a plan to the EPA very soon."

Eric made a new column and wrote the word "RESPONSE," then continued. "So, Big Chem comes back and requests some time to analyze the problem, and the EPA says they'll give them four months to answer the EPA demands. Big Chem says, they will comply with the request, but asks for six months more to do so. EPA says they will grant three months additional but not six. Big Chem ignores the EPA and seven months later Big Chem presents its proposal for correction and cessation. Keep track of these moves, people."

Eric wrote the word "Proposal" under the RESPONSE column, put the chalk down and turned toward the class. "Now, the EPA says it will take the Big Chem proposal under advisement. Big Chem requests an answer within two months. EPA says it may need a longer time for fair evaluation and when the end of the day finally arrives, Big Chem has a plan under consideration for clean up, but has not ceased polluting."

Some of the students were chuckling now as Eric sped on like a stand-up comic. "The EPA fines Big Chem $2.5 million dollars and takes them back to court for violation of the cessation order and subsequently files again for failure to clean-up the serious methyl chloride run-off problem. And, just as the song says, the beat goes on and on and on. See, the fines are cheaper than cessation and proper clean-up."

The students were quiet. They understood. Eric continued. "So, there it is. The problem isn't just one of science. It's about human behavior. Indifference, lust for power, greed and in the final sense, of inhumanity. You might think that I am acquiescing, but in light of the way the system works, that first young man was absolutely right. Most of the graduates of our school will go on to become part of the problem, not part of the solution. Maintaining the status quo."

In the back of the hall a man stood up and said loudly, "You people are listening to rubbish. Absolute rubbish. The EPA does an excellent and honest job. Your teacher is an ill-informed radical. A heretic. Listen to him at your own peril." The man stumbled up the steps and stomped out of the lecture hall amid scattered murmurs from the students.

Without responding to the accusation, Eric continued. "I can only tell you that as long as we do nothing to stop these huge corporations, they will continue to pollute. The EPA is playing dangerous games with our health, and worse, the health of future generations. They know what they're doing to us is wrong and they know the pollution conditions across this country and the world are very severe. Unfortunately, power and money rule the day. I know for a fact that the houses and offices and cars of the elite have been protected from air pollution and the food they eat and the water they drink are tested to ensure they are always the very best and safest. They certainly don't want to die, but sadly, they don't care if we do."

Another student raised his hand and asked. "In light of these allegations, what chance do we have to stop the bad guys? It seems as though it's them against us. And I'm not even sure who the 'them' is exactly. The people who work for the companies that pollute? The people who run the companies that pollute? The people who own the companies that pollute? The people who buy the products of the companies who pollute? Plus, whoever 'they' are, they're pretty good at what they do. They have all the power. How can we fight something that big and anonymous?"

Eric scratched his head. "Yeah. Well, I don't have a definite answer to that one. I should have, but I don't. The first thing that comes to mind would make me sound like an anarchist, and I'm certainly not an anarchist. No. I'm not sure what to do. Has anybody got ideas?"

The class was quiet. These young scholars were really giving some thought to the question.

After a minute, another hand went up and the student spoke out. "We could form groups, then assign each group to a different corporation, petition those corporations constantly until they correct the problems and parallel to this petition process, we could keep bugging the EPA to keep hounding the corporations and then we'd deliver the story, current updates and results to the media. A barrage."

Eric responded. "Yeah. That's what the Sierra Club and *Greenpeace* do and that certainly might begin to bring it to public light. But, we all know that people have a very small attention span. After a while it just becomes more noise and people lose interest. Corporate patience is long, and strong. They'll just wait out the media storm, and still do nothing. A good idea, but I think more is needed. You're close, Trish. Very close, but no cigar!"

Eric perched on the front of the lab table. "Up until the eighteenth century, most of the pollution was natural. Volcanoes, floods, fires, tornados, hurricanes, all natural causes. But as man found new technology he unknowingly, assisted nature. In doing so, he compounded the natural disasters, thereby causing even greater pollution. Very rapidly his technology increased and then he caused his own manmade disasters. Because of innate greed and lust for power and control of nature, he ignored the results. Pollution was born."

Eric slipped off the lab table. "Okay, my earlier instruction to do a paragraph of definition and description of the effects on that list of chemicals, the 'Dirty Dozen,' is withdrawn. You don't have to do it. What I do want is for you to come in to this hall with an open mind and begin to think about our earth as a house you live in. It's very dirty. How are we going to clean it up?"

Eric looked at each of the eager young faces, and then in his most profound manner told them. "Tomorrow we'll begin to explore the mind-boggling amount of pollution man is creating and what effect it has on our environment and ourselves. Prepare to be shocked, amazed and horrified! How you understand the problems and begin to think of how to solve them is a huge task. The future and the natural balance of the world, unfortunately, is in your hands."

With a smattering of applause, the students quietly left the lecture hall. Eric hoped that he had inspired them to think seriously.

The next day the lecture hall was completely full. "Many more than yesterday," he thought. "Beginning to do SRO business. Maybe I'm gonna be a hit!"

Eric took his place behind the lectern on the table. "Good morning people. Good to see so many of you. Today, I'm going to give you more to think about. Here in America we like to make important lists. You know, *Forbes* richest, top 40 hits. So we're going to look at the top environmental disasters."

Eric went to the blackboard.

"Along with deforestation, changing the flow of rivers and streams, polluting the land, water, air and food, man—in his inimitable style—has created significant disasters and injured the environment in some very dramatic and unnecessary ways. Here are a few oldies, but goodies:

"The Great Dust Bowl of the 1930s is still considered one of the worst environmental disasters in the United States. Yeah, it was man-made, for sure. Farmers didn't listen. Years of growing the same crops with no care about erosion, resulted in the wind stripping five inches of topsoil from over ten million acres. It lasted an entire decade. The loss of topsoil is estimated at 4.8 billion tons. The resulting death and sickness are inestimable. Greed, and pure stupidity."

Eric was writing on the blackboard and talking very fast.

"The 1947 Texas City, Texas disaster was an explosion aboard *The Grandcamp*, a docked ship in the harbor. The explosion was caused by an unnoticed fire on board the ship. When left unattended, it caused 3,200 tons of ammonium nitrate fertilizer on board to explode. The subsequent fires and explosions were referred to at that time as the worst industrial disaster in America. Nearly 600 people lost their lives and several thousand were injured. The blast was felt as far as 25 miles away.

"The 1967 Valley of the Drums. Now this one started with the discovery of thousands of leaking drums of industrial paint waste on 23 acres of farmland outside of Louisville, Kentucky. It was found that the owner of the land had dug several pits and for years had been dumping the toxic waste in order to re-use the barrels again. The EPA came into the picture and the owner covered the open pits to prevent them from being seen. The EPA analyzed the property and creek and found high levels of heavy metal, polychlorinated biphenyls, and some 140 other chemical substances. Two large aquifers remain contaminated to this day.

"The 1969 Santa Barbara Oil Spill. A blow-out from an off-shore oil rig. Six miles off the California coast on Union Oil's Platform-A. An estimated 100,000 barrels of crude oil spilled into the channel and beaches of Santa Barbara fouling the coast line from Goleta to Ventura. This spill is ranked just behind *The EXXON Valdez* spill in 1989.

"The 1975 Love Canal. The rate of tumors, miscarriages and birth defects in people living in the area around Love Canal, New York was unusually high. No wonder. Since the early 1940s Hooker Chemical had been pouring its chemical waste directly into the Love Canal. It's estimated that before anyone got wise they had dumped almost 22,000 tons of chemical byproducts. But before they got caught, they covered the site with dirt and grew grass to cover up the toxins below. They were even going to build a school on top of it. But they were found out. The area was deemed uninhabitable and the sickly residents of Love Canal simply moved away.

"The 1988 Chevron Oil Refinery in El Segundo, California. For decades, the refinery had leaking pipes and tanks that dumped some 252 million gallons of oil and millions of gallons of chemical-laden waste water into the huge aquifers under the refinery. Water safety in this area is still an issue.

"The 1989 Exxon-Valdez spill in Alaska. A new ship, *The Exxon Valdez* hit Bligh Reef and ruptured its cargo tank. This oil, 10.8 million gallons, spilled into Prince Edward Sound. It caused huge pollution to the ocean, damage to the animals and birds, human deaths and they are still cleaning up the oil mess on the beaches."

Eric concluded. "That's enough of mankind's record of avoidable disasters caused by greed and stupidity for today. This is just the short list of a few of the environmental disasters that have happened in the United States. I assure you, there are many, many more. Tomorrow, we'll take a look at two particularly active corporate polluters."

Eric dismissed the class and the students filed out without much discussion. No one had pulled together all of this information for them before. It was a punch of reality that would take a while to sink in for them.

Five

A Young Ignorant Audience

Again, the old lecture hall was packed. Signaling for them to be quiet Eric began.

"Now just multiply the number of biggest accidents we talked about yesterday by ten, by the number of influential industrial nations in the world, each who have their own top disasters, and you can see the work you have cut out for you as professional environmentalists. It's a hell of a mess. And sadly, it's getting worse, not better. We are poisoning our own people and are just as cavalier and careless throughout the rest of the world with our new technology and our terrible toxins."

Eric picked up a group of papers.

"I've been following this story in India. It's getting no attention here. But it's a prime example of how two big U.S. corporations are blithely perpetrating incredible damage to people and the environment and profiting from it."

Eric passed out some notes to the class. "There was a Union Carbide chemical spill in Bhopal, India not so long ago, in 1984. I think this will eventually be considered the worst man-responsible disaster in history, if it ever gets the light it needs for people to learn about it. The final decision is still being stalled, even though the evidence is irrefutable."

Eric went back to the blackboard and drew two vertical lines making two wide columns. At the top of one column he wrote UNION CAR-BIDE and on the other DOW CHEMICAL. "These are all-American companies that you know very well. These two companies have one of the lengthiest records of damaging the environment, poisoning people, animals and plants, manipulating administrative rules and regulations, and generally dodging the law throughout the world. It's not just the US that doesn't take real action against these serial polluters; no country in the world dares challenge them. So, there are no consequences for the bad acts of these corporations."

Eric started making a list from his notes on the board. "So, here is a quick recap of the environmental record of Union Carbide and Dow Chemical. You've got these notes in your handout, so don't waste time writing. Read through this list. I want you to think about this. Let's take a look at the facts. They are very shocking."

Eric used an overhead projector to display the notes and read them aloud to the class.

UNION CARBIDE:

1930: 476 Carbide workers die of silicosis while construct-ing tunnel in Hawk's Nest, West Virginia. 400 death claims settled for just $130,000.

1955: At Carbide's gas diffusion plant at Oak Ridge, Ten-nessee, about a million kilograms of mercury leaked into the ground, water and air. Almost half the workforce showed high levels of mercury in urine.

1973-78: Benzene gas leak at the Peñuelas, Puerto Rico; propane gas leak at Institute, WV; explosion in polyethylene plant at Antwerp, Belgium; electrocution at an Eveready plant in Jakarta, Indonesia.

1980: U.S. Departments of Labor and Health & Human Services report high brain cancer rates at seven petrochemical plants including Union Carbide's Texas City facility, where 18 workers had died of brain cancer. And, Union Carbide is fined $550,000 for air pollution violations dating back to 1972 at its Yabucoa, Puerto Rico graphite electrode plant.

1981: Union Carbide is fined $50,000 for spilling 25,600 gallons of propylene oxide into the Kanawha River, West Virginia. And the Indonesian press reports high mercury levels in wells and rice fields around Union Carbide's insecticide plant.

1982: Hydrogen chloride leak in Union Carbide's Massey yard at South Charleston, West Virginia; several hundred residents evacuated. A tank containing acrolein explodes at Carbide's Taft, Louisiana plant; 17,000 people evacuated, property damaged over a 1.5 mile radius.

1984: Union Carbide is fined $105,000 for hazardous waste violations in West Virginia.

1985: Union Carbide is notified by the U.S. Environmental Protection Agency (EPA) that since 1980, 190 chemical leaks occurred at its Institute, West Virginia plant, including 61 leaks of methyl isocynate (MIC), 107 leaks of phosgene, and 22 leaks of both. The EPA seeks $3.9 million penalty from Carbide for delayed reporting of skin cancer tests involving diethyl sulfate. The tests showed high rate of skin cancer in mice treated with the chemical. And 5,700 pounds of acetone and mesityl oxide leaked from Carbide plant in South Charleston, West Virginia; dozens of area residents are taken ill. The EPA fines Carbide $212,500 *for producing a new chemical at its Sisterville, WV plant. Toxic leak at Institute, WV facility injures workers and local residents. $88 million in damages sought, Carbide pays $4,400 fines.*

1986: The U.S. Occupational Safety & Health Administration (OSHA), inspects Carbide units at Institute, WV and finds 221 violations of 55 health and safety laws, proposes $1.4 million in fines.

1987: Union Carbide agrees to pay $40 million to clean up its Uravan, Colorado uranium contamination, and to pay the state $2.8 million in legal costs. And, Union Carbide pays $408,500 to settle 556 health and safety regulations violations at its Institute and South Charleston, WV plants.

1988: Union Carbide sues 115 insurance companies to recover the costs of cleaning up its hazardous waste sites. And, the explosion of 4,300 pounds of ethylene oxide at Institute, WV; tetranaphthalene spills into Kanawha River.

1989: Union Carbide, one of three defendants in an asbestos cancer lawsuit, settles for $900,000. EPA imposes penalty of $325,000 jointly against Union Carbide and Rhone-Poulenc Ag Company for water pollution from Institute, West Virginia facility.

1990: Carbide's Institute, West Virginia facility leaks methyl isocyanate (MIC) gas and muriatic acid, injuring 7 workers, after which 15,000 residents ordered to remain indoors. And, Mexican environmental agency SEDUE takes action against Carbide's Kemet subsidiary for illegally dumping hazardous waste.

Eric marked in the "Union Carbide" column on the board: WORLD-WIDE POLLUTER! "Union Carbide is a serious polluter. You noticing a pattern here? None of these places are affluent centers of education and culture. And if you think Union Carbide is bad, look at this world renowned chemical giant."

DOW CHEMICAL:

Radioactive Contamination: From 1951 to 1975 Dow ran the hydrogen bomb facility at Rocky Flats, Colorado. A series of fires and incidents of leakage from stored radioactive materials took place in 1957, 1959, 1967, 1969. High levels of tritium and plutonium were found in the surrounding areas in the 1970s. They still haven't paid anything.

Agent Orange: During the Vietnam War, Dow became infamous for providing two of the most horrendous weapons used against the Vietnamese people: Agent Orange and the napalm bomb. US Air Force sprayed 76 million liters of various herbicides over forests and crops. About two-thirds of it was Agent Orange, manufactured by Dow. About 3 million Vietnamese were affected with cancers and other diseases. While 150,000 newborn babies have deformities, Air Force crews who handled the poison suffered similar effects. US veterans filed lawsuits and in 1984, they were awarded $180 million damages. Attempts by Vietnamese people to claim similar damages were rejected by US courts.

Dioxin: The main manufacturing site and headquarters of Dow are in Midland, Michigan. For years, at least until the 1970s, Dow was dumping various chemicals into the Tittabawassee and Saginaw Rivers. It wasn't until the 1980s that high levels of the cancer-causing dioxin group of chemicals were discovered up to 35 kms downstream from the plant. A lawsuit by residents is still suffering delaying tactics in Michigan, while EPA is negotiating with Dow for cleaning up the poisoned sites.

Dursban: This best-selling pesticide of Dow is a lethal nerve poison, chlorpyrifos, which is to this day available for most home and garden uses. Poisoning incidents are surfacing, but Dow's advertisements make all kinds of safety claims and this poison is marketed worldwide as far as India. Can you guess how Dow has persuaded officials to authorize its license for marketing their 'insecticide' products in India?

Breast Implants: In the last ten years, the rising controversy over whether silicone gel-based breast implants made by Dow Corning causes health issues, including cancer, resulting in thousands of lawsuits and class action suits claiming compensation for rupture complications. So far, scientific studies have been inconclusive.

DBCP: Another dangerous chemical used to destroy worms in banana plantations. Workers in DBCP production units were rendered sterile by it. After successfully winning claims against Dow, use of DBCP was banned in the US in 1979. But Dow continued to export it to Latin America where there are now allegations that the Dole Food Company used it extensively in plantations with chilling results. Plantation workers rendered sterile have filed law suits. Third world victims cannot win cases easily in the US, against US based corporations. Not a big surprise.

Waste Dumping: The EPA has named Dow as one of those liable to pay for clean-up of 96 sites where hazardous waste was dumped by Dow and other companies over several decades. These are called Superfund sites.

Eric wrote in the Dow column: WORLDWIDE POLLUTER! "I won't bore you with the statistics on Bayer, BASF, Monsanto and the others. You can research them yourselves. They're all big polluting criminals, too. But, again, look at what just two companies have done. They have a long, long history of doing harm. Is this the kind of thing that can be stopped?"

Eric looked out at his student audience. Their eyes were on him. But, the students were pessimistically silent.

Eric launched. "There are many other methods to achieve the same profits. The basic industrial chemical processes haven't changed for a hundred years. These products are still dangerous and cause great pollution during their production. These companies can, and should do better. They really know how to correct these faults. But they don't! The EPA fines and fixes? Government intervention to stop the mess? Bull shit! It just never happens. They don't care. They kill more people, the CEOs get bigger paychecks and the shareholders get larger dividends, and that's a fact. It's just plain greed!"

There were no responses from the students. Eric leaned onto the lectern and dropped his head for a moment, then looked up. "Well, now. All of this has worn me out. I promised you more, and there will be more. Tomorrow we'll take a look at how 'they' are poisoning our food and water. That information will make you sick. Then, I hope it will make you mad enough to take action. The food people are the kings of lying."

Eric gathered his notes and plopped them into his briefcase. "End of lecture. All over. Everybody out of the pool. See you tomorrow."

Every student in the lecture hall stood up and applauded Eric. But it wasn't their approval he was after.

Six

Preparing to Inform Them

That night he and Elaine had a quiet dinner at home, enjoying each other and not talking of teaching or world events. Just small talk.

As they were having dessert, Elaine said, "Eric, a big box came for you by UPS today. What's in it?" Elaine got up and struggled to bring in the big box.

Eric was on his feet and quick to help her.

"What the hell is in this box, fucking bricks? It's heavy."

Eric pulled the box to the table and they both sat back down. "Not even close. It's books. I ordered two hundred paperback copies of Upton Sinclair's *The Jungle* for my kids."

"Okay, I won't ask why. After all, it is your allowance, so spend it the way you want."

Elaine was the most unique woman he had ever known. Classy and dignified one moment; next swearing like a sailor; often practical, then becoming tempting and sexy.

She continued. "But why *The Jungle*? It's so gross and disgusting and most of them probably read it in high school."

"Yeah, maybe. But, kids at the age I am teaching are eating machines. They'll eat anything and usually do. They've been taught to trust what they eat and really don't know how the food got into the grocery or in the package or fast food restaurant. They probably think that all food is squeezed out of some kind of, well, a food machine. Part of my job, as I see it, is to inform them of where the food originates, how it is processed, and how much of the food we eat has been adulterated for various reasons. And some of the additives cause bad things to happen when eaten by humans. Cancer in the stomach and intestines, kidney and liver problems, immune system reactions, hormone disruption, et cetera. I want them to know."

Elaine got up and took his hand. "…all right, all right, no more talk. Time to call it a night. Come on now."

Next day, the lecture hall was again filled. Eric's "show" was becoming very popular.

As he entered the hall, the students applauded.

Instantly Eric wished he had a musical theme to accompany his entrance. "Such enthusiasm! And without a warm-up act!" He smiled as he reached the front of the room. "Hello and welcome to another meeting of the people who are going to change the world!"

The students cheered.

"A change is certainly needed. What if I told you that 98% of everything you eat and drink could ultimately kill some of you. I said some of you, because the "additives" in our food effect people differently, and sometimes not at all. But first, why do our food producers use additives?

Eric didn't leave much of a pause, but there weren't any hands going up in the air, so he continued. "Many reasons, but mostly because of profits. You don't have to care about who gets sick, as long as you're making money. Greed."

A few groans from the students inspired him to change tactics a bit.

"Okay. It's still the 'them again against us' theme, but this time it's very personal. It's the food we eat! I want you to see where your steaks, hamburgers, hot dogs, pork chops and chicken sandwiches come from. I've got a very interesting video for you. The pictures and narration tell a very sad story. We will watch and hear the story, and then we'll talk. Kill the lights and roll the film."

Narrator: The ideas of happy animals living on farms where cows forage on green grass and chickens roam free in the fields is very far from reality. The animals that we eat lead unhappy lives in confined overcrowded facilities called "Factory Farms."

Narrator: Animals raised on factory farms have had their genes manipulated and are pumped full of antibiotics, hormones and chemicals to support increased productivity. In the food industry, animals are not considered animals at all. They are called "food-producing-machines."

Narrator: The chicken industry produces 6 billion chickens a year for slaughter. This industry is ruled by only 60 companies which have created an oligopoly. Broiler chickens are selectively bred and genetically altered to produce bigger thighs and breasts, the parts in most demand. The birds are bred to grow to their market weight of 3 1/2 pounds in seven weeks. The growth hormones and antibiotics fed to chickens are passed on in their flesh, which when eaten, will be retained and effect the immune systems and hormones of humans. The growing conditions can cause salmonella and e. coli, which can be passed on to humans.

Narrator: There are about 250 million layer hens in U.S. egg factories that supply 95% of the eggs in this country producing over 6.5 billion eggs, annually. These layer hens are subjected to constant light to encourage greater egg production. At the end of their laying cycle the hens are either slaughtered or forced to molt by water and food deprivation, which shocks them into another layer cycle.

The growth hormones and antibiotics fed to chickens are passed on in their flesh, which when eaten, will be retained and affect the immune systems and hormones of humans. Their growing conditions can cause salmonella and e. coli which, again, can be passed on to humans.

Narrator: *90% of pigs suffer both physically and emotionally when they are confined in narrow cages. Many pigs become crazy with boredom and develop vices like fighting and cannibalism because of their frustration. They don't see daylight until they are shipped for slaughter. The growth hormones and antibiotics that are fed to pigs are passed on in their flesh, which when eaten, will be retained and affect the immune systems and hormones of humans. In addition, this environment causes toxic gases from the pigs' waste that encourages a number of diseases and illnesses, including pneumonia, cholera, dysentery, e. coli and trichinosis, many of which can be passed on to humans.*

Narrator: *Dairy cows are bred today for high milk production. Over 20 billion gallons of milk is produced in the U.S. each year. For cows who are injected with Bovine Growth Hormone, their already high rate of milk production is doubled. Dairy cows produce milk for about 10 months after giving birth so they are impregnated continuously to keep up the milk flow. When cows become unable to produce adequate amounts of milk they are sent to slaughter. Many cows are fed growth-promoting hormones, appetite stimulants and pesticides, fertilizers, herbicides and aflatoxins that collect in the animals' tissues and milk, which when consumed, will be retained and affect the immune systems and hormones of humans.*

Narrator: Beef cattle are the staple of the American diet. Over 27 billion pounds of beef are produced each year. 98% of the cattle are raised in feedlots that are close to the slaughter and packing operations. The conditions in these "meat houses" today, have great similarity to those conditions that existed over one hundred years ago in Upton Sinclair's The Jungle. *These conditions are not only inhumane to the animals but extremely dangerous to the workers. These places are some of the biggest OSHA and USDA violators. Again, the beef cattle are fed growth-promoting hormones, appetite stimulants and pesticides, fertilizers, herbicides and aflatoxins. E. coli bacteria collect in the animals' flesh and tissues. When this meat is consumed by humans, all the additives and e. coli will be retained and affect humwn immune systems and hormone levels.*

Narrator: Why all the preservatives in our food? Common antimicrobial preservatives include calcium propionate, sodium nitrate, sulfites and disodium EDTA. Benzoates are used primarily in acidic foods to prevent bacterial growth. Sulfites can cause allergic reactions. Monosodium glutamate (MSG), can cause headaches, nausea, weakness, difficulty breathing, drowsiness, rapid heartbeat, and chest pain. BHA and BHT are common preservatives with questionable value as agents to prevent oxidation and rancidness. Common preservatives injected into food include formaldehyde, glutaraldehyde, ethanol, methylchloroisothiazolinone. Fresh foods are always better, but huge profits are involved in holding our food for the longest refrigerated, frozen, packaged and bottled shelf life possible. The side effects of these preservatives in our food are constantly debated, but generally their usage is agreed to be necessary. Necessary for great profits for the manufac-

turer. Greed is the enemy of mankind. Greed and a lack of humanity.

Eric turned the lights back up and walked to the front of the lab. "Well, I really don't know where to begin. The film said it all. Shannon and Tara, will you give one of these books to each person? I hope we have enough. If not, after you read it give it to someone else to read. The book is called *The Jungle* by Sinclair Lewis. Many of you may have read it in high school. Please read it again with the understanding that the same greed and indifference to both animals and humans has existed for a long time, and it's still with us."

Eric surveyed the room. There were lots of side conversations among the students. Speaking up, Eric continued. "It's sufficient to say that these industries need to clean up their ways of doing business. They need to use some of their obscene profits to create natural, sustainable growing conditions and more humane slaughter methods for the animals as well as safer conditions for their workers. They need to stop adding growth hormones, and antibiotics to the animals and stop adding preservatives to the final products just to extend the shelf life. These all pass from the flesh of the animal to human beings."

Eric stopped to make sure the students were paying attention, and then spoke slowly and carefully. "They need to provide us with truthful labeling. They need to stop lying to us. Their enormous greed is slowly killing us all. We need to get real mad at them, and demand that..."

A young man entered the lecture hall interrupting Eric, and passed him an envelope. Eric opened it. It was a handwritten note.

Professor Atkins—

Please dismiss your class and come to my office, immediately.

—Dean A.J. Davis.

The class seemed to sense that something was amiss.

The look that formed on Eric's face verified their suspicion. Eric folded the paper and addressed them. "Wow. This is *déjà vu*. I'm back in high school again. I've been called to the principal's office!"

The students laughed at his joke.

"Well, today's meeting of the 'young radicals' is over. Read that book and look up some of the stuff we've talked about. It'll make you sad to be an American. And tomorrow, be sure to bring muskets and gunpowder and your good brains with you, because we *will* continue this important discussion of what to do, and how we might do it."

The class soundly applauded Eric as he left the hall.

"Called to the office!" Eric thought. "How ridiculous. Teaching? Creative ideas? Points of view? Free speech? Not in this Nazi institution! What bull shit."

Eric entered the Dean's office without knocking. He was very upset. "Listen Davis…"

"Sit down, young man. You and I are about to have a serious talk." The Dean said in a phony autocratic tone.

Eric wasn't having it. "Now look here, A. J. First, I'm about eight years older than you and a tenured professor. Second, about my teaching: I'm not knocking a particular company, just trying to get my students to understand that the application of ecology is not just simple science, the politics and social science involved must enter the equation. I mean, not to look at…"

A voice in the shadows from the corner of the room cut him off sharply. "You mean corporations, like Big Chem, Big Oil and Big Food. The same corporations that produce jobs, energy, life-saving medicines, consumer products, not to mention, making great contributions to this university. They are really the bad guys? No. I think not."

Before Eric could ask who this man was, Dean Davis interrupted. "Look here, Eric. You've lost your way, again. Oh, you're a brilliant scientist and a very good teacher. But you can't just go flailing about with your wild accusations. These are impressionable young people. We're here to lead them into the world with sound ideas, not fill them with thoughts of anarchy."

"Anarchy?" Eric immediately realized that his lecture hall had been bugged or infiltrated. He wondered if all he had been saying was on tape and filed away under "Potential Terrorist." He attempted to regain control and stammered. "D-D-Dean Davis, I'm only trying to enlighten these young minds. If you'll only..."

"Professor Atkins. Enough!" Dean Davis was adamant now. Be silent, please. Now, here's what's going to happen. At the beginning of your class tomorrow you will announce that you are going on a sabbatical to rest and gather research for a book that you are writing. You will say goodbye to your students, dismiss them, and leave.

Eric was stunned.

"I truly want you to take some time away to get refocused, and when you come back, I want a change in your teaching manner. Or I want your resignation. Is that clear enough for you?"

Eric sadly nodded his head in consent and left the room.

As he walked down the hall, he thought. "Suspension. And I might be expelled. It is like high school. Who was that man in the shadows with the attitude? Ugh, this teaching shit is getting to me. I'm tired and frustrated and angry."

He stopped in his office, picked up the phone and dialed. "Freddy? Eric. You out of class now? Good, meet me at *The Hole*. I need a beer and someone to talk with. ...Thanks. See, ya."

Seven

Heroes

The Hole was the bar and lounge area of the old *College House Hotel*, just off the campus of Hardeston University. It was the favorite gathering spot for the professors.

In a back booth, Eric and his longtime friend Professor Fred Masinga sipped on big glasses of house-brewed beer. Fred Masinga was a professor of chemistry at Hardeston and, like Eric, a Vietnam veteran. Fred had never married. Though he often sounded quite serious and proper, Fred was a confirmed playboy bachelor who liked to party. Eric had known him for years. They were good friends; almost like brothers. Eric trusted Fred.

Eric set his empty glass to the side, raised his hand and extended two fingers to the waitress. She got the message.

Fred finished his glass and nodded in agreement.

"Freddy, I've been sacked. Well, not really sacked, but told to take a sabbatical and clean up my act. Change my ways or I'll be canned."

"What have you done to piss-off Big Brother now, Eric my boy? Telling it like it is again? Trying to teach the little kiddies the truth, instead of the corporate propaganda?"

"You got it, bud. I wish I'd never taken this stupid teaching job. Shit, they have more rules than the government. What am I saying? They are the government, aren't they?" Eric took a deep breath, closing his eyes for a moment. "I'll go away and come back as ordered, and try it again. One more time, I guess."

The beers came again and Eric continued. "I'm not naive. I know what the deal is. The corporations fund the university and the government funds the university so they both feel that they have the right to control the curriculum and edit the facts as they see them. Today it starts in grade school and goes all the way up. They're-writing history, giving the students erroneous facts and statistics. And then they wonder why none of these kids can think, or create, or even read half the time. I guess *they* just want workers, not workers who can think critically."

"How right you are. But what are we to do? It's a huge system, and I think it's been this way a long, long time. We've both tried the corporate world. No difference out there. Just more 'watch what you say' and 'watch what you do.' None of that is real freedom, in this land of the free, is it?"

"Not by a long margin. If you do contradict the powers that be, you get censured, or worse. Fred, what I found out when I worked at AP&G Oil would shock and enrage the public. Okay, I did some general speaking out, but the public will never know all of it. The people that are sick and dying and dead from the pollution, from the rampant oil refining. It's monstrous; unconscionable."

Eric was talking loudly now. "How can you get it across to the people, the general public, that more and more of them will eventually die from the greed and carelessness of these big corporations? That corporations don't care! Why are we treating corporations like people, giving them more rights and freedom than individual citizens? Freddy, how do you catch and keep the public's attention so they can learn? Maybe it's impossible. For every cable talk-show, or blog, or book that might try to tell the truth, the goddamned corporations buy more advertising on TV and magazines and newspapers, write their own blogs and books, do their own talk-shows and use their spin-doctor-PR agencies to continually tell the public more lies. The public buys it. They'll never hear the truth. Never!"

Freddy touched his fingers to his lips and said, "Shuss. Shuss. Hey, Eric. You're beginning to rant. Slow up. Take a slurp of beer between those angry tirades or you'll burst a blood vessel. Calm down."

"Okay. Okay. But I'm getting older, you know? This is very serious for me. I truly want to do something meaningful. And I don't know what to do, let alone how to do it. It's frustrating, Freddy!"

Freddy looked at Eric and spoke very seriously. "Look, my friend. Outside of blowing up everything and everyone involved with those polluting corporations and liquidating the EPA and most of Congress and the wealth that controls them, I don't see what you can do. Never thought I would say it, but we may have lost our right to dissent. They may have won this round."

"Bull shit. They've only won if nobody opposes them. Where is that revered American fighting instinct? That guy that says: I don't buy it! The guy that will talk-up and write letters and make calls and speeches, or march on Washington? Where the hell did our fighters go?"

Freddy was up to the question. "Oh, that fighter is out there. But today, he isn't going to do any of that. He doesn't want to lose his job, or find that he suddenly owes a big tax bill, or is placed on a watch list, or maybe even gets put in jail. No, no. That cantankerous American man is still around. But he'll only speak out at home—or quietly in a bar. You know. Quietly, Eric."

"All right, my friend. I get it. I'm still talking too loud. I'll lower my voice so the establishment sympathizers don't turn me in. Dammit, Freddy. This is driving me crazy. There is an answer to almost everything. I will find the one that belongs to this problem, I promise you."

Freddy changed the subject. "So where will you go for your little vacation? Going to take Elaine with you, or see if you can score some strange?"

"I don't need no strange, my good man, Elaine is plenty for me. You know, I don't have any idea where I might go. Out of this area, that's for sure."

"Well, I might be inclined to tag along with you, if it's someplace interesting. Spring vacation is coming up, you know. How about visiting the oil-spills in Alaska? I hear they're in bloom and lovely this time of year."

"You shit-head. I don't know where I'm going. I'm just beginning to think about it. I'll let you know when I figure it out." Eric emptied his glass and called for another round. "I'm gonna have to go after the next beer. I've got lasagna and Elaine waiting for me at home."

"Sometimes I envy you, Eric. A loyal, loving girl. Marriage. Familiar. Secure. I might try it sometime. Longest relationship I ever had was a full semester with that beautiful adjunct professor from New Jersey. Remember? You know, that statuesque dark-haired girl? When she didn't get offered the full-time gig, her love went out the window. What a shame. She was hot!"

The chitchat went on for another beer and neither of them mentioned governments, or universities or pollution. Just good friendly talk about anything and everything.

Eric reached across the table and flipped up Freddy's stylish tie. "You're such a fop. Always dressed in the best. Pretentious manners."

"Always got a lot of girls with that shit." Freddy grinned and straightened his tie.

"Always actin' like you're high born..."

"Hey, careful...high born from the south side of Chicago. I can still do you in, brother."

They clinked the heavy beer glasses laughing, then drained the last of the beer. Eric asked for the check. Both of them shook hands and hugged like they would not see each other again. The men parted not wanting the night to end.

Eric and Freddy had met-up at a VFW post in San Diego. Both were in college at the time. They drank a lot of beer and became fast friends.

Eric believed Freddy was about as smart a man as he had ever met; tops in the field of chemistry. Freddy's Marine training in covert activities got him interested in chemistry. They taught Freddy to mix "things" into poison and scar and blow up the enemy; wicked things. The stories in 'Nam of "Fiendish Freddy," as they called him years ago, made Eric's skin crawl even now.

Now Freddy was on the other side. A devoted chemical ecologist, he had developed many antidotes to the poisons that man was putting into the environment.

Eric was barely in the front door at home when the phone rang. He answered. "Eric Atkins. …Yes, Dean Davis. …Yes, I am going away. …I don't know where, but I am going. …Yes, I'll let you know the details when I've decided. …Yes, Dean. I promise. I will call you before I leave and let you know all. …Okay. Good bye."

Elaine, standing nearby, looked puzzled. "Why does he want to know where you're going?"

"Not sure," Eric said, giving her a big bear hug. "He's sure adamant about my leaving. Anal bastard."

Elaine pulled away. She shot a look at Eric, and then walked into the kitchen.

Eric hung up his coat. "The Dean is a dufus. A real nitwit!"

After dinner with Elaine, Eric called Freddy.

"Freddy, here. Missed me that much, eh?"

"Yeah, can't live an hour without you. Big Brother Davis called me before I even got in the front door. Freddy, he wants me to call him and tell him exactly when and where I'm going."

"Sounds to me like something is triggered to happen when you leave. New professor, I imagine. Wants to make sure you're gone. Doesn't want you to get to the new man, to influence him or prep him…"

"Yeah, I guess so. But his demand for details is outrageous. ...I'll probably know more tomorrow. I'll call you after. Night."

The following morning Eric pulled into his parking space at the university. He grabbed his briefcase and headed across the lawn toward his office. It was a hot day. He took off his sweater and stuffed it into his case. Ignoring the "Keep Off The Grass" signs, he walked through the spray of the sprinklers.

In his office, Eric put together some cardboard boxes and surveyed the things he'd accumulated during the many years of his teaching at Hardeston. It was bittersweet.

He talked out loud to himself as he packed up his books and papers and memorabilia. "Those are the visionaries," he said pointing to the framed pictures hanging on the wall. His heroes: John Muir, Rachel Carson, John Lilly, Roger Revelle, Jacques Cousteau, Ralph Nader, Al Gore, and a picture of Eric and Captain Paul Watson. "But Paul Watson is my kind of guy. He's not just talking. He's doing something about the problems: *acta non verba*. He's the man."

Eric gathered some notes and headed for the copy room. He knew he would probably get into trouble again with Dean Davis by talking about his heroes to his students, but he thought, "What the hell. I'm already busted." Maybe an introduction to these true giants might encourage the students to learn more, and inspire them to act.

With great excitement Eric entered the hall for his last lecture. He noticed that every seat was filled and many were sitting in the aisles. "Guess the word is out," he thought.

Eric took his place in front of the class and set up his notes on the lectern placed on the long lab table. "Well, hello," he shouted to the murmuring crowd.

It took a moment for everyone to quiet down.

Eric looked out at the packed lecture hall. He took a couple of deep breaths, then began. "Today I want to talk to you about my own heroes and where my own inspiration comes from. I hope you'll find out more about them yourselves. First, Captain Paul Watson. I know this man. I sailed on his ship, *The Sea Shepherd*. I believe in and support his work. He is one of the great heroes in the fight against the destruction of our oceans. You can find out more about him in the library."

Eric shuffled his notes, nervously, and then looked out again at the crowd. "Captain Watson defines himself as a sort of 'eco-pirate.' He's committed to aggressive, passionate interference with what he sees as the organized destruction of the planet's oceans by the agents of profit and greed. Since 1979, he's sunk nine outlaw whaling ships and rammed numerous illegal drift netters and tuna boats."

Eric held up his hand at the audible gasps. "In doing so, he was complying with the law as defined by the UN General Assembly in 1982." Reading from his notes he continued. "I quote: 'States and, to the extent that they are able, other public authorities, internal organizations, individuals, groups and corporations *shall safeguard and conserve nature* in areas beyond national jurisdiction.'"

He let that sink in. "That's all of us. Mandated by the UN General Assembly. Now, Watson believes that, at the moment, the most important weapon that can be deployed to ensure that the plundering of the high seas doesn't take place—any guesses?"

No one volunteered an answer.

"—is the camera. Remember that old phrase, 'Light is the best disinfectant?' Captain Watson teaches that it's important that the public be informed at all times. He believes that actions like his are required to uphold existing laws. He is very clear, though: these are not acts of political or philosophical protest. He believes that the solution must be non-governmental. It's up to all of us."

Everyone shifted uncomfortably in their seats.

Eric gathered his packet of notes, walked around to the front of the lab table and leaned back against it. He set his notes off to the side and changed his tone. "As you may, or may not know, this will be my last class for a while. I'm taking a sabbatical to continue research for a book that I'm writing, tentatively entitled, 'Pollution: Who Did It? Can We Find Them and Stop These Evil Morons From Doing More?'"

The hall burst into laughter, breaking the tension. Eric waited for it to die down. "Seriously, though. On this last day, I want to introduce another great man, my dear friend, John Lilly. He is a mentor and has given direction to my life. I met Dr. Lilly just after I quit being the 'flunky-boy' for big oil at the AP&G Oil Company in San Francisco. I was still searching for what I wanted to do with the rest of my life."

Eric slid up onto the lab table. "God, I was an angry young man... newly married, suddenly without a job and a little scared. I needed direction and grounding. My meeting up with John Lilly truly changed my life. The times that I talked with him were not only thought-provoking, but extremely educational. Lilly is the kind of man who inspires you to see things in ways you just could not have imagined without his perspective. He made me think; really think. He's made contributions in the fields of biophysics, neurophysiology, electronics, computer science, and neuroanatomy. And he invented and promoted the use of an isolation tank to study sensory deprivation. His research so far includes the physiology of high-altitude flying, physical structures of the brain and consciousness, human-animal communication. He developed instruments for measuring gas pressure..."

Eric paused. He closed his eyes for a moment. He was rambling and he knew it. He struggled to find a focus. "Dr. Lilly has so many questions about mankind and about life in general. He's still exploring possible answers. His research into the physical structures of the brain and consciousness are some of the most fascinating things you'll ever read about. He's written more than a dozen books. He's a sensitive human being, always open to discussion if you're truly interested."

Eric stared out into the sea of people. He knew he hadn't grabbed them yet. He changed tactics. "John Lilly has spent years investigating human-animal communication, especially the intelligence and communicative abilities of cetacea—whales, dolphins, porpoises. His work helped create the United States Marine Mammal Protection Act of 1972. And…he was the model for the George C. Scott character in *Day of The Dolphin*. That movie was loosely based on the experiments he did, privately at first and then, to his chagrin, under the auspices of the U.S. Navy. When he discovered that the Navy just wanted to use his dolphins as floating weapons platforms, he ended his marriage with the military."

He stopped for a moment. Now, the crowd was paying attention.

"As I mentioned before, it was Dr. John Lilly who invented and promoted the use of an isolation tank as a means of sensory deprivation, in order to study human consciousness. His deprivation chamber was also funded by the Navy. Lilly learned that the human mind reacted strangely when it was without sensory input. He did years of work on the possibilities of imposed mental regression and of the effects that could actually be documented. Check out that study. It's fascinating. This 'deprivation chamber' research was the subject of another movie, *Altered States*. I recommend that you rent *Day of The Dolphin* and *Altered States*. Not only are they entertaining, but quite thought-provoking… And we do want to provoke thinking, don't we?"

He had them now. Popular culture. Entertainment. Always gets their attention, Eric mused.

Eric veered back toward the subject matter detail. "John was always involved with how the brain worked, both in humans as well as terrestrial and oceanic mammals. He was probably the first to equate brain size to mental capabilities. John Lilly held that since we humans came from the ocean, we were definitely related to all of the large mammals that still resided out there and if we could only communicate with them, we could learn a lot from each other."

Eric pulled his legs up onto the cool marble lab table and crossed them, lotus style. He picked up his notes and sailed on. "From experiments showing that a human's brain size and that of a dolphin were about the same size, Lilly postulated that each should be able to calculate at about the same speed. He hypothesized that the orca, or so-called killer whale, which has a larger brain, would calculate even faster, and therefore the brain of the sperm whale, as the largest cetacea, would calculate the fastest. He further proposed that if brain size was a measure of fast calculations, then the larger the brain, the more stored knowledge it might contain."

He stopped for a moment to let this sink in. "Remember, most of the ocean species have been here for millions of years—a lot longer than any human species. Imagine, then, if these marine species, the cetacea, could learn our language, and we theirs, what we could discover about our own origins. Only in this last century has man captured dolphins and killer whales instead of killing them. Lilly believed that this new exposure to man from land would give the cetacea new and comparative information which they could then share with others of their species when they were returned to the wild. He believed they should be as eager to learn about us, as we are about them. He wanted reciprocal communication."

The hall was silent.

"It's a great idea, isn't it? Capture as many cetacea as possible. Attempt to communicate with them. Allow them to observe mankind on land, close up and then return them to the oceans. Well, that's what John Lilly wanted to do. Unfortunately, their return to the sea seldom occurs. The cetacea have become our captives for exhibition."

Eric put his notes down. "Lilly was also involved with the effects of psychedelics and hallucinogenics. He is friends with and collaborates with Dr. Timothy Leary. They were the very early stoners—for medical and experimental purposes, you understand."

Knowing chuckles popped from the crowd. "Ultimately, Dr. John Lilly was and is trying to understand how the brains of mammals work. He's accomplished a lot during his lifetime. Another great example of not just talking, but doing."

Eric jumped off the lab table and grabbed some handouts and sent them through the crowd. "I've taken the liberty of excerpting passages from the introduction of Dr. Lilly's book: *Communication Between Man and Dolphin.* I encourage you to read the entire book. I'm not going to read all of it to you, I'm just going to hit the high points so you can hear about Lilly's ideas in his own words."

Eric read the following out loud:

Man is changing the planet. He has a history of killing off all of the large mammals of the land. The large mammals of North America and Africa are being decimated by man. In the seas the pelagic mammals are being critically depleted as man invades and hauls their bodies ashore for his purposes.

We need a new ethic, new laws based on those ethics which punish human beings for encroachment on the life-styles and the territory of other species with brains comparable to, and larger than, ours.

Those who believe that they are killing to provide huge reservoirs of flesh for industrial use rather than killing the largest, most sophisticated brains on this planet, somehow must change their beliefs; their killing must be prevented by giving the Cetacea the same legal protections as humans.

I envision the day when the current oceanaria will progress from being "prisons" for dolphins, to being interspecies schools, educating both dolphins and humans about one another.

The Cetacea are sensitive, compassionate, ethical, philosophical, and have ancient vocal histories that their young must learn.

Cetacean knowledge of humans is restricted to experiences in the sea between the Cetacea and human ships of warfare, yachts, catcher boats, and so forth. Very few, if any Cetacea have experienced man on land then return to the sea to tell the others of their species anything about we humans. Yet, the Cetacea have come to realize that man is incredibly dangerous in concert. It is such considerations as these that may give rise to their behavioral ethic that the bodies of men are not to be injured or destroyed, even under extreme provocation. If the whales and dolphins began to injure and kill humans in the water, I am sure that the Cetacea realize that our navies would then wipe them out totally and at a faster rate than the whaling industry is doing presently.

Thus, we deduce that the whales have a knowledge of man, fragmentary as it is, which they weave into theories and into accounts of direct experiences in a way similar to the way we develop knowledge of one another.

They probably, because of their large brains, have extremely long memories and the capacity to integrate these memories equal to, and better than our own.

Seventy-one percent of the surface of our planet is covered with oceans, inhabited by the Cetacea. Let us learn to live in harmony with that seventy-one percent of the planet and its intelligent, sensitive, sensible, and long surviving species of dolphins, whales, and porpoises.

It is hoped that the coming generation will recognize that that is probably one of the greatest and most ennobling challenges that face man on this planet today. To be able

*to break through to understand the thinking, the feeling,
the doing, the talking of another species is a grand, noble
achievement that will change man's view of himself and of
his planet.*

—Dr. John C. Lilly, *Communication Between Man and Dolphin*

The students were quiet for a moment and then applauded in a most
respectful way.

"Paul Watson and John Lilly and Jacques Cousteau, too, are against
the rampant pollution of our air and land and oceans. They are definitely
in opposition to mankind's wholesale dumping of his refuse and trash
and manufactured poisons into the oceans, or having it buried in landfill
environments. John Lilly has first-hand experience of what pollution is
doing to the planet and he doesn't like what he's seen. He's inspired a lot
of people, like Al Gore and Ralph Nader."

Eric paused for a second. "Ralph Nader. Now there's another guy
who started on the right track. He's spent years writing and speaking and
lobbying and fighting in courts for better ecology. I think Ralph's heart
is a good one. He hasn't changed his tune much. The big corporations
and their greed are rapidly killing us all and Nader's Raiders fight them
at every turn."

Eric walked back behind the lab table to the lectern. "And why, I
hope you are asking, does man hurt man? Why does he do these things?
Well, believe it or not, even with the best scientific intentions, the honest
and great desire to help mankind and to bring new and better technology, all the good is ultimately cancelled out by one thing: Greed. That's
why 'rush to market' are the most important words in the corporate
world. Most of these disasters, deaths and sicknesses could have been
prevented. The corporations needed to take more time to evaluate the
effects of their products and projects made in haste, and the toxins they
produce. Before anything is manufactured, and absolutely before distri-
bution, these corporations should know and communicate the answers to

whether their products will damage the atmosphere, or ruin our drinking water; whether these food preservatives and additives will ultimately hurt or kill people. Will these miracle drugs and medicines have side effects that will kill or maim those that use them? We all need to ask whether all these products are necessary?"

Eric was ready to launch now. "Our great centers of knowledge, like this university, unfortunately mill out unthinking and really uneducated students, because they, too, have become a business. No longer are they merely places of learning. Today, they are funded by the government, which is funded by the big corporations. Universities, too, have become pawns in an ongoing and enormous game. And greed is the root of it all."

The students were with him, now. He could feel it.

"Corporate greed is insidious. The ruthless determination employed by the owners and operators of these corporations is diametrically opposed to the truth. They have no integrity. They don't care. As long as the product or process turns a dollar and gets to market quickly, no matter what the cost in human suffering, they're happy. They are truly corrupt in what they do."

Eric looked at the assembled students and visitors and spoke loudly. "But now, it's your duty to put a stop to these greedy, malicious corporations. Join every activist group you can. Learn the truth. By getting involved you may be able to stop the pollution and save lives today, and you will definitely ensure that tomorrow, future generations will have safe and healthy lives, good food, clean water and air."

The auditorium burst into cheers and applause.

From the back of the hall, Dean Davis stormed down the center aisle toward Eric. He walked behind the lab table and spoke quietly to Eric. "That's quite enough, sir. You've been warned. No more radical talk!"

Dean Davis then turned to the class and spoke loudly, tamping down the continued cheers and applause. "How can I apologize to you young people? Professor Atkins is not well and has said some strange things lately. Not his usual good teaching, and certainly not representative of Hardeston University, I assure you. But take heart, he will be going off on a little vacation and will come back rested and refreshed. Upon his return we will all be glad to see him. Today, however, this class is dismissed and will resume tomorrow with Professor Chatsworth as your teacher. Everyone go now."

No one got up. The boos and catcalls unnerved Dean A. J. Davis. He stood for a moment just staring at the unruly students. He turned and gave a stern look to Eric, then quickly exited through the side door of the lecture hall.

Eric held his hands up for quiet. "Okay, I guess you know why I'm going away, don't you? Well, with that kind of pressure and hassle, I really do need a vacation. Not only is that fat little bastard rude, but he's 180-out most of the time. You guys just keep your good brains open. Look for the truth and don't believe anything until you've researched it yourselves and if all the research and teaching smells like shit, it probably is. I'll see you soon."

The students were on their feet, stomping and applauding and cheering. Dean Davis might have been right in one respect. These kids were impressionable and with a little dose of the truth they became eager to rebel. If these young people formed a movement, they would give the establishment big trouble.

Eric shook hands with almost every kid in the hall on his way out. Lots of "good lucks" and "piss on the dean" and "we love you" and "hurry back." Eric had experienced Andy Warhol's "fifteen minutes of fame" and he liked it.

Eight

The Firing

Back in his office, Eric finished putting papers, books and notebooks into several boxes. Two of the boys from his class stopped by and asked if they could help him take the boxes to his car. With these eager young helpers, the task was done in no time. He thanked them and picked up his office phone and called Elaine.

"Hello sweetheart. ...Yeah, I got all my stuff together. Couple of nice kids helped. ...I'll be coming home right away. ...Say, give Freddy a call and tell him I want him to come to dinner with us tonight. ...And tell him not to bring anybody. This is a family dinner. I want to talk privately. ...Okay. Love you too, baby. See you shortly."

Eric chose the finest restaurant in the area, *Walken's By the Sea*. He requested a large table in the corner near the windows overlooking the ocean. The full moon was just coming around and it danced on the calm sea as the waves lazily splashed against the rocky shore. The candles on the table and the low-key lighting of the restaurant made a perfect romantic picture.

Each of them ordered to their liking. Eric told the waiter to take his time with the courses. Wine was poured and the conversation began to flow.

"This is great, isn't it?" said Eric. "The two people I love most, a great view, fine wine and a delicious dinner to come. Who would want more? You can kill me now. I'm happy."

Elaine nuzzled up to Eric and whispered. "If you're going away, love, you need to give me plenty to remember you by. And I mean plenty."

"Two love-birds." cracked Freddy. "Have you no sense of decorum? No shame? Making love in public... No class at all. How pedestrian."

Eric snapped back. "Listen bachelor-boy, you're just jealous. And by the way, while I'm on vacation stay away from my wife, you hound."

Freddy winked at Elaine. "Oh, I will, Eric. I will. I promise." Freddie winked at Elaine again and smiled that big toothy grin of his. "So, lover boy, have you decided where you're going on this forced exile of yours?"

"Yeah, I have. Going out on my boat, the *New Horizons*. I'll sail around for a week or two and try to discover what I was doing when I stopped doing what I was doing."

"That's a great idea, Eric." said Elaine. "I only wish I was going with you. I love that boat. We've had some great times out there, haven't we, babe."

"Mmm-mmm-mmm. Yes, indeed we have." Eric snuggled into Elaine once more, nuzzling her neck.

"Ugh! Now you're just showing off." Freddy modestly looked away, trying to change the subject. "So tell me what happened on this, your last day. Did Dean shit-head leave you alone?"

"Freddy, my boy, it was straight out of a movie. The place was packed. Even people sitting in the aisles!

"You're a rock star!" Freddy added enthusiastically.

"I got about halfway through my very well-prepared lecture on John Lilly—if I do say so myself—and I'd just barely mentioned, Al Gore and started to talk about Ralph Nader, when Dean 'Dufus' came bounding down the aisle. To be fair, I may have attempted to incite the students to take action, but nothing specific. He told the students that I was not myself, that I was going away and they would see me soon, but now the class was over. Well, they booed and hissed and called him names and I think he peed his pants, 'cause he raced out the door like the devil was after him."

Freddy laughed. Elaine was a bit more cautious.

"And the students loved it. As I was leaving they all came up and shook my hand and wished me well. They're a good bunch of kids."

"Tremendous! Now that is a first-class conclusion to a wretched affair. I don't know how you keep your temper. You're a better man than I, Gunga Din," Freddy offered enthusiastically.

"You've certainly taken a lot from Dean Davis lately. No more about that man or that school tonight. Okay? Let's just have some fun." Elaine wasn't quite sure what to make of things yet. She knew, though, that Eric needed a change of perspective.

The dinner courses came. The wine flowed and they ate good food and laughed and had a wonderful evening, enjoying each other's companionship. It was a family affair.

As the coffee and after-dinner liquors came, Eric became serious again. "I can't stop thinking about the Atlantic Pacific and Gulf Oil Company. Those guys are criminals. I do want to hurt them, but I can't figure out how to do it."

Freddy replied. "Money, money, money, money! Nothing else matters to them. Bad publicity, controversy, a drop in the stock market, fading confidence by their beloved investors. You must destroy their money. That'll hurt the greedy bastards where they live. Yeah, give 'em hell whenever you can, but you have to make them lose money!"

The next day, late in the afternoon, Eric decided to go to the beach. The sound and sight of the ocean always helped him think and focus his thoughts.

He parked the car, kicked off his shoes and walked along the warm sand. The sun was descending in the western sky. It was going to be another beautiful sunset.

As he looked out over the ocean, he saw six or seven dolphins bounding in and out of the water. It looked like they were playing. The dolphins were so beautiful and graceful that he wanted to run right out in the ocean and join them in their life of freedom.

Eric sat down on the beach and stared at the ocean. The sun was very warm, but for some reason, he was remembering a cold evening in Michigan, many years ago with his oldest friend, Clay Perkins. It was the winter of 1973. They were at the movies. The last scene of the feature film *Day of the Dolphin* was concluding. The film starred George C. Scott, who was one of Clay's favorite actors. The credits rolled and the audience got up from their seats and began to file out of the small-town movie house into the chilly air.

Eric and Clay sat in their seats watching the credits roll as the auditorium emptied. Finally, they got up, buttoned their coats and silently left the theatre.

It was one of those fiercely cold winter nights in that little Michigan town. The snow fell lightly onto clumps of hard frozen ice piled all along the sidewalks and streets from a previous storm. White vapored breath-puffs emanated from the people leaving the theatre trudging back to their homes.

Eric and Clay, their heads bowed in thought, silently walked together down the snowy sidewalks, crossed the street and headed toward the neon of a corner bar.

Once inside, they brushed the snow off of their clothing and mumbled orders to the bartender. They sat for a while sipping their drinks, staring pensively into the large mirror on the back of the bar, quietly thinking about the movie.

The pop music of 1973 played on the jukebox. Most of the patrons of the little bar were perfect pictures of the time and style of the *Age of Aquarius*.

Clay removed his ball cap and unbuttoned his GI Marine coat and began to relax and enjoy the warmth.

Eric spoke. "So, what do ya think he said, Clay?"

"What? What did who say? What are you talking about?" Clay was not on the same wavelength.

Eric calmly restated his question. "The dolphin. The dolphin. What did he say to George Scott when they were both in the water? What did the dolphin say?"

Clay did his best imitation Oliver Hardy. "Stanley, I don't have the slightest idea what he said!" Clay picked up his ball cap and tipped it toward Eric. "I don't know. Make war, not peace. Or is it the other way? Hell, I haven't got a clue."

Eric laughed. "Actually, I think you got it right the first time. Make war."

Clay became serious. "We shouldn't have screwed around over there in 'Nam. It's really bad. Guys are dead 'cause nobody will escalate our little outing to a full-scale war. Politics prevail. Death and madness and confusion every day. It's the shits, man!"

"Thank God, I stayed alive, thanks to you."

"All in a day's work. *Hoo-rah!*" Clay took a long pull on his drink.

"You saved my life a time or two as I remember," Eric said. "When I got out, I went to school. I actually learned a lot. I like what I do for a living."

Eric was still a PFC when he got out in 1970. He went on to college and married Elaine. He was very happy.

In 1971, Clay had mustered out as a First Lieutenant with an honorable discharge. He had done some very hard time in Vietnam, was wounded and got a Purple Heart. He'd used his VA benefits to complete his education and go to law school.

Clay responded to Eric. "Yeah, I like what I'm doing, too. I've got a decent job. I'm happy, too."

Eric's focus changed from the memory of the dark interior of the bar to the very present setting bright sun over the ocean.

A few years after seeing that movie, the great John Lilly had given Eric his answer to what the dolphin might have said. Eric had Lilly's note laminated in plastic and had carried it in his wallet all this time. He took it out and read it again.

Why was he thinking of Clay Perkins? Eric wondered where his old friend might be? He had tried, with no luck, over the years to find him. Clay might even be dead.

The sun was going down. Eric walked back up the beach, slid into his car and drove home. On the way, he began to itemize what things he would take with him on his trip.

At home, he remembered his promise to call Dean Davis. Reluctantly, he dialed the Dean's number. "Dean Davis. ...Eric Atkins, here. ...Fine and you? Great. I promised to tell you when I was going on my little vacation. ...Tomorrow, early in the morning. ...I'm going out on my boat. I'll sail for a while and think it all over, as you suggested. ... Yeah, it's a beautiful boat. I named her *New Horizons*. ...No, I keep her down at the Billings Marina. Nice people down there. They've always treated me well. ...Certainly. When I come back my wife and I would love to have you and Mrs. Davis aboard. ...No, I'll probably be gone a week or ten days. Just want to cruise about, you know. ...Yes, I'll call you when I return, Dean Davis. ...Thank you. Good night."

Elaine came up behind him as he hung up the phone. "Why does he need to know everything?" She slipped her arms around him and squeezed hard.

"Big brother...." Eric sighed. He turned and pulled Elaine to him, lifted her face up toward his and kissed her passionately.

Nine

The Sabbatical

That night Eric fitfully fought off a surreal dream. He saw himself speaking to a large audience in an auditorium. He warned them that if the environmental and ecological problems were not solved, it would inevitably result in an end to mankind. The audience was very responsive to what he was saying. They began to shout: "Blow-up the polluters! Kill them all!"

In the middle of his speech, a group of black uniformed men burst upon the stage. Two of them grabbed Eric's arms and hauled him away. A portly man in a black uniform then addressed the audience. "Eric Atkins is a trouble-maker. He is an anarchist and a terrorist. Those of you that listen or act like him, will go to jail with him. Go home, now. Go home…" The speaker was fat and ugly with melting features.

Eric was still able to recognize the antagonist of his dream. It was Dean Davis.

Eric awakened in a sweat.

Elaine was there beside him and tried her best to comfort him.

"That bastard Davis. He's even in my dreams. Who is he really working for? He's no educator. He's the traitor! He's an establishment puppet. What time is it?"

"Eric. Calm down. It's twelve o'clock. It was just a nightmare. Go back to sleep, darling. I promise, you'll have better dreams. Think of happier things, baby."

It was five o'clock in the morning when Eric and Elaine pulled the car up to the docks. In the darkness, the moist air of the marina seemed very cold and cut through Eric's jacket right into his bones.

He always liked to arrive at the boat near dawn. It made it feel more like the old buccaneer movies. "Arggh, Lassy. We'll be leavin' with the mornin' tide," he said to Elaine, using his best caricature of a pirate.

Elaine smiled and helped him remove the two duffel bags from the trunk of the car. Eric slung one of the bags over his shoulder and before he could get the other one up, Elaine gave him a long kiss and held him very tightly. Elaine wanted him to go…but then again, she was worried about him going.

Eric loved this woman very much. Elaine was a good reason to keep on living and to happily sail back home.

Elaine had ensured that there was plenty of food, bottles of water, vitamins, a full first aid chest and lots of clean clothes for Eric. Eric had spent most of yesterday afternoon loading the provisions on the boat. He had everything he needed.

Eric had added a box filled with scotch whiskey and bourbon, a mixed case of white and red wine, two cases of beer and a large baggie filled with some very fine Thai buds. With all those goodies, he might end up sailing in circles, but on this voyage, he was all set to tune-out, and turn on.

Carrying one of the bags and dragging the other, Eric moved down the long dock toward his slip. Eric stopped under the dim lights in front of the *New Horizons*, his 85-foot power sailboat. This was something he had wanted since his childhood back in Michigan and now he had it. He had purchased this vintage boat for a song. For two long years he did most of the repairs and refitting himself. Today, the boat that he bought for twelve thousand dollars was appraised at over one hundred thousand dollars. Sweat equity was a good thing.

Elaine really wanted to go with him and normally she would have. But this time, Eric just wanted to be alone and take his time. He needed this trip. The job-pressure was making him tired and irritable. He'd needed this opportunity to rest and relax for a very long time.

Eric turned and waved goodbye to Elaine. At the end of the pier, through the fog, she appeared as a phantom. Her cheery goodbye echoed across the marina and seemed like a ghostly and ethereal voice.

Eric waited and watched the car's tail lights fade into the misty darkness. Except for the slapping of the waves against the boat, all was quiet. Eric was alone. It was eerie.

He set the sea bags on the dock and jumped aboard to turn on the deck lights. Then he went back to the dock, picked up the bags and hauled them, one at a time, onto the boat. He unlocked the hatch and took the bags below, then came topside and readied the boat to set sail.

In the mist, Eric saw three bummy-looking men propped up against the wood pilings about two slips down from his boat. With baseball hats pulled over their eyes, they seemed to be sleeping. Eric couldn't really see them well in the fog and darkness, but one of them had his eyes open and was observing Eric with great scrutiny and interest.

Eric took a large cooler chest to the far end of the pier to an ice machine and filled it with ice. When it was filled, the chest was too heavy to carry, so he dragged the huge box using its wheels along the pier and up to the boat.

One of the men yelled, "Hey, you need any deck hands on that fine boat?"

Eric was startled, but composed himself quickly and responded, "Afraid not, buddy. Just a quiet cruise by myself. A few days alone."

"No room on board, eh? Not even for the man that saved your life?"

"Saved my life?" That voice! Eric dropped the chest and moved toward the man. "Whoa, wait! Clay Perkins? Is that you?"

From the mist Clay responded, "*Hoo-rah!*"

Excited, Eric headed toward him. "Well hell yes you can come on board!"

Clay gestured in the direction of the other men.

Eric hesitated. "Uh. Okay, sure, sure. Come on, all of you."

Clay kicked one of the men. "Hey, you birds, get up."

The three of them headed toward the boat and followed Eric.

"Where have you been, Clay? Come on you guys. Let's go below and have a drink. This calls for a celebration."

They went below decks. The interior of the boat was quite luxurious. Eric opened his well-stocked liquor cabinet.

"How'll you have your drinks, boys? The usual, Clay? See if I can remember. Bourbon, neat, with a water back. Right?"

Clay nodded at Eric and then winked at the other men.

"And yours, gentlemen? Say, my name is Eric." He stretched out his hand to the other men.

One of the men stepped forward and shook Eric's hand. "Charlie's the name. And he's Bob. Always glad to meet a friend of Clay's. Whiskey neat. Twice."

Eric started pouring, "So, Clay, where ya been these years? It's been a hell of a long time. What have you been doing?"

Clay kicked back on one the bunks and sipped his bourbon. "Hmm... Where to start?"

Eric offered, "Well, did you get that big corporate job?"

Clay took another sip. "Not exactly. After law school, I interviewed with all the big law firms and major corporations, IBM, General Motors, you name it! I was determined not to jump at the first good offer. I wanted to hold out for the biggest and most lucrative deal, the one with the best future. I took a job with a law firm, Bif-Bof & Bam, who represented just about everyone except the Pope. They had offices all over the world, in twelve countries. I set about to make my mark and amass a great fortune. I did make lots of money. Lots of travel. Lots of wine, women and song."

Clay took a long drink, emptied his glass and handed it to Eric for a refill.

Charlie and Bob sat quietly in the background, eyeing their surroundings.

Clay sat up and continued. "Then one bad day, bingo! I'm up on charges of money laundering, tax evasion, organized crime, and racketeering. Oh Christ, it was a mess. I beat the criminal charges, with a little help from some very good attorneys. But I lost my ticket. I was disbarred. Kicked out of the club."

Eric handed Clay his refill and slid into the bench of the galley table with his own drink.

"When you're trained to do law work, that's all you know. That's how you think. I was dead in the water. I started to drink…maybe too much, but I needed not to think, you know? I couldn't keep a job. Finally quit trying. Dropped out." Clay got up, downed the bourbon in one gulp, slid into the bench opposite Eric at the galley table and slammed the glass down.

Clay turned and gestured at Charlie and Bob. "And here I am today with Charlie and Bob. You know, they have stories they can tell, too. We were all once men of means and influence. Sad story, eh?"

Clay turned back and looked Eric in the eye. "So. Enough about me. Your turn, bartender. What have you done with that new life that I gave to you?"

Eric was a little overwhelmed. "Well, that'll take some time. Hey, I've got an idea. What are you guys doing for the next few days? Can you take some time for a little travel?"

Clay, Charlie and Bob laughed, uncomfortably. "Uh, let me check my schedule," Charlie snickered.

Eric, embarrassed, replied. "Right. Stupid question. Well, let's call it a holiday. You three are my guests here on the *New Horizons* for a whirlwind cruise through the southern coastal waters of the mighty blue Pacific Ocean. Deal?"

The other two men looked at Clay. He nodded yes.

Eric was a little overexcited. "Okay, you landlubbers. Rig the mooring arm, shiver your timbers and we'll shove off for adventure on the high seas!"

They all shot Eric a puzzled look.

"All right. So, I'm not Captain Blood," Eric said. Bring the bottle, come topside and relax for a while. We'll use the engines to leave the harbor. We'll put up her sails when we get out to sea."

The sun was just coming into view as the beautiful boat moved quietly through the harbor and out to the open sea. On Eric's orders, the men helped Eric put the sails aloft, each following his commands like experienced seamen. In reality, they were all little boys again, playing pirate games.

Eric set their course to south-by-southwest and locked the wheel on autopilot. Then, he turned to address the men with his best Errol Flynn impression. "All right, me scurvy mates. On this trip out, we're all men of means. So, go below and get out of those clothes and hit the head for a shower and shave. Then get into some nice clean clothes. Plenty in the lockers below. Help yourselves. And when you return topside, throw those stinking, shitty clothes overboard."

After cleaning up and changing clothes they came up again for drinks and sat casually on the deckchairs. The shower, shave and new clothing had changed these bums into decent looking respectable men once again.

One of the men had clamped on earphones and was listening to a portable music player. The other was reading a book. These gentlemen of leisure were enjoying themselves to the fullest.

Eric and Clay settled back and continued their talk. "Now this is the good life, Clay. Smell that air. It's great to be alive!"

"Yeah. So, what is it that you do to afford a raft like this? You must be doing all right."

"Well, I've had my ups and downs. When I got out of the corps, I moved to California and went back to school. I majored in biology at UC

Riverside, then got a masters at Berkley, then a PHD in oceanography at The Hardeston Institute Of Marine Biology. Worked a little, got married and…"

Eric stopped. "Say, Clay. Do you remember that movie we saw? You know, the one with the dolphin? Turns out the character George C. Scott played was based on a true-life person named John Lilly, who was also a marine biologist."

"Interesting…" Clay took a quick look around, fixing his eyes on the whereabouts of Charlie and Bob, then turned his attention back to Eric.

"Yeah! Lilly is an amazing guy. I read about him and then I looked him up in Malibu. I actually got to meet with him a few times. He's sometimes a little outrageous, with some crazy ideas, but he's a real genius."

"And that helped pay for this raft how?"

"No. No. It didn't. After I got my masters I thought I'd join Jacques Cousteau and do something meaningful. That didn't happen, but I did get involved with *Greenpeace*. By then I'd already sold out to a big corp, Atlantic Pacific and Gulf Oil Company. I thought I could help the ocean environment by watching over those thieves in the refining and offshore drilling business. God, those bastards would totally wreck the ocean if they had their way. Greedy sons of bitches!"

"Uh-huh. So that's how you paid for this boat?"

"Kind of. That job paid very well, but I… I needed to do something more meaningful. Clay, I got into their 'secret files' and started to write little articles telling the truth about all the 'accidents' and doing some public speaking about the oil companies. They didn't like it."

"Naturally." Clay replied neutrally.

"Long story short…"

"No longer possible, pal," Clay snickered.

"Asshole. They fired me. I'd put my dough away, though, and made some good investments. I got married…"

"Married? Who'd have you?"

She's a beautiful woman—Elaine Kroslin. You'll love her, Clay."

"Kids?"

"Uh, no. We did try. But I've got problems that came from…I don't know. Maybe Agent Orange in 'Nam. We stopped trying. Maybe it's best. If we did have kids they could have all kinds of problems…you know?"

Both men were silent for a moment. The tiny white waves lapped at the boat.

"So…" Clay interrupted. "You're not working at anything anymore? Just a man of leisure?"

"Not exactly. I was happy with Elaine, but I felt unfulfilled. So, I decided to teach ocean biology. It was a big cut in pay, but I wanted to do it. I tried the obvious curriculum and teaching methods, but recently I started to tell the truth about the oil companies and chemical companies to my students. I think they were really interested and wanted more. But, my boss, Dean Davis, got very angry and invited me to take a vacation, or quit. So here I am. Not sure where things are at the moment."

Eric looked away for moment, and then back at Clay. "So, what's really going on in your life now, Clay? You guys were in pretty rough shape when you came on board."

"Master of the obvious, as usual. Well, I'm broke. Down on my luck, as they say, just like Bob and Charlie. They lost their jobs, good jobs, and couldn't ever get started again. Ended up like me—out in the cold. One day up, the next down, and there we were sitting on the street wondering what the hell had happened. The only real luck is that not a one of us has ever been married. No kids no ex-wives to take care of. In fact, Charlie and Bob have no family at all. Parents are dead. No relatives. They're really alone in the world."

Clay stood up and walked up to the rails, his back to Eric. He looked out over the ocean lit only by the moonlight, and took a long deep breath. "We decided a couple of weeks ago when we first met to become the three musketeers. We're all 'professional' drinkers, when we can get it. We've got that it common. And we enjoy each other's company. You've done a good thing for us all, Eric, taking us on the big sail with you."

Eric got up and slapped his old buddy on the shoulder, and stood beside him, staring out at the ocean. "It's nothing, my friend. Look. I don't want to pry, but I'm gonna. How the hell did you get in this shape? I know what you told me, but how could this have happened to you? You were never the screw-up. And you were sure not the type to quit. What's really going on, Clay?"

Clay jerked himself away from the rails and flopped back on the seats. He kept himself turned away from Eric. "I told you what happened, man. No insult, old buddy. But I really don't want to talk about it right now. That's that."

Eric put up his hands. "All right. All right. Talk whenever, if ever. Just know, I'm your friend, man."

Clay took a sip of his drink and spoke slowly. "I know—I found out the hard way, I should say—there's no difference between the big corporations and our government. They're the same. The corporations tell those in the government what to do and they all look upon us little citizens as just a source of cash flow. We're revenue to them. They consider us like the military does, allowing for collateral damage. The bean-counters help them justify that a certain number of us can starve, be poor, be without housing or jobs. A certain percentage of physical damage won't hurt the bottom line, whether it's natural resources or human resources. I can tell you from firsthand experience, if something isn't done, and done very quickly, there's going to be a massive social breakdown in this country. It's splitting apart."

Eric concurred. "All fueled by greed…In terms of the environment, the oceans, this planet is doomed if we can't stop man's destructiveness. I'm with you, pal."

Clay looked Eric in the eye. "Eric, if you could, how would you propose to accomplish a clean-up? I mean, you're talking about billions of dollars, even if they stopped polluting today."

"Well, you can't really do a clean-up until they stop polluting altogether. I've been writing and speaking about this for years. I thought that might get these corporations to stop. The EPA fines them. They countersue the EPA. It gets locked in court battles for years. The EPA wins, the corporation pays the fines, promises to clean up the mess and to use less polluting manufacturing methods in the future. They don't keep any of their promises and the EPA cites them again. And the process goes on and on. The corporations have built in the legal expenses and fines as a cost of doing business and just pass it on in inflated product prices to the consumers. It's totally insane. We're paying for these bastards to slowly murder us and kill our future generations, all in the name of corporate profits!"

Charlie and Bob were still drinking heavily and laughing to themselves at the other end of the boat. They had no interest in the intense conversation that Clay and Eric were having.

Clay agreed. "Yeah, it's a conspiracy. So tight between the corporations and government. And you can't get the public or the media to even begin to address it. But, Eric I ask you again: if you could, just a little game now, how would you fix it?"

Eric stared off at the ocean again. "Well, since legislation and law enforcement haven't and probably won't work, and you can't get the public excited about the slow poison that's being given to them, only one of two choices, as I see it. One, continue to wait and hope that the evil, greedy bastards in the corporations and the government get some human conscience. Or two, develop a group of people who believe in the justice of the cause and then, just like we used to do to the enemy in 'Nam, surgically remove each problem, systematically."

Clay straightened his back. "You're talking about taking the law into your own hands, then?"

Eric turned around and faced Clay, leaning his backagainst the guard rails of the boat. "Well, I'm not saying it's right, but it may be the only way. And, in some cases the damage they've already done is irreversible. But, it has to stop. We're only here a short time and the pollution and damage that we're causing and have allowed to happen for the last two hundred or more years... Ugh. Yes, now that I'm openly talking about it, I think radical, forceful action must be taken!"

Bob staggered over toward Eric. "Hey, Cap'n. D'ya have any more scotch, my man? We're runnin' dry."

"Yeah. Sure," Eric answered him. "You guys can really put it away. You should go easy. It's gonna be a long time before we can get more." Eric stopped for a second. "Oh, what the hell. I've got plenty below. Keep that fire burning, Clay. I'll be right back."

Charlie joined Bob and they both came over to Clay's chair.

With a wink and a thief's glint in his eye, Bob whispered to Clay, "Where did you find this mark? This is heaven, Clay. Think he has any cash money on him? I found some jewelry downstairs. Probably more stuff down there, too, eh, Charlie?"

Charlie grinned like a fool.

"Look, you bozos, we don't commit the robbery 'til we can get out of the ocean. Do you guys know how to sail this thing? I don't. Anyhow, out here there's nowhere to run. We'll hit him when we get into port, okay?"

The two men thought for moment and signaled their agreement by giving sloppy salutes to Clay.

Eric climbed back up with another bottle of scotch for Bob and Charlie. "Here you go, fellas. This should hold you for a while."

Charlie and Bob grabbed the bottle and slithered back to the other end of the boat, snickering and laughing.

Clay faked embarrassment. "Wow. I guess I should apologize for those idiots, but..."

"Not necessary. *Mi casa, su casa* and your *amigos*, are *mi amigos*." Eric looked out at the black expanse, surveying the ocean all around them. "This looks like as good a spot as any to throw down the anchors for the night. I'm too drunk to drive anyway. Stay seated, Clay. It's as simple as pushing a button. All automatic. I'll be right back."

Eric moved to the wheelhouse and slowed the engines, and eventually shut them down and let out the sea anchors.

Eric came back out and Clay helped him drop the sails and batten down all the rigging for the night. Finished with their work, the two men continued to drink and talk into the night. The clear evening sky with billions of stars overhead and the calm ocean gently rocked the ship; the perfect backdrop for two old friends to re-unite. In this setting, it was easy to go back and forward in time. Eventually, they made their way below and collapsed into the bunks in the sleeping quarters.

Charlie and Bob continued to drink into the night until they, too, collapsed on deck.

Around 8:00 a.m., Eric came topside. He kicked at the two men until finally they awakened in a drunken muddled mood. "Hey guys. Nice soft bunks down below. Come on I'll show you."

The drunken men stumbled and grumbled as they went below decks. Eric kindly put them to bed.

Eric noticed Clay was lying awake in his bunk. "Ready for some breakfast, ol' buddy?"

"Some coffee for sure. Got any danish?"

"Just happen to have some. Or you can have bagels and cream cheese, you name it."

They made their way to the galley area.

Clay sat across from Eric as he prepared the food and coffee. "Sure did talk and drink a lot last night. Just like the old days, Eric. You know, I don't even have a headache. Must be the salt air. I feel great!"

"Good times. Hey, I'm really glad you're here, man. Long time coming."

They sat a while sipping coffee and looking out the windows onto the beautiful day.

"Eric. I've been thinking. Would you really do something about the pollution problem, if you could? I mean was it all just talk with you or would you risk your life and everything you have to stop these bastards?"

"Whew. You always wake up with a bang like that? No wonder you're not married."

"Ha ha. Well, would you?"

Eric thought seriously for a moment. "Yeah. I think I would. I'd put it all on the line. But if we protest too much, make big waves, we'd just fall into their trap. They'd arrest us and put us in jail and still nothing would get done. I've thought about it a lot. The world doesn't need another martyr, it needs results. Hell, buddy, I'd gladly die if I actually made some kind of a difference before I bit the dust! Grab your coffee and let's go topside."

They moved up the stairs to the aft deck of the boat and sat down in captain's chairs with a small table between them, looking out at the ocean.

Clay was solid and serious now. "Okay. I wanted to wait until we were both sober, like now, before I told you what I really do for a living. I'm with the CIA."

"Yeah, and I'm the king of the world…CIA? And I suppose those two are FBI agents?"

"No, no, no. They are as they seem. They're real bums."

Eric shook his head. "You aren't makin' any sense, man. Are you serious? What is a CIA agent doing out with a couple of bums…on my boat?"

"I need to get out of the Company. These guys are part of my plan."

"What?"

"And…so are you, Eric. You know, the government's been tailing you for years. There's a contract on you."

Eric stood up and looked at Clay. "Whoa. Whoa. Wait a minute…"

"Did you really think that those inflammatory articles and speeches after you left the oil company landed nowhere? You got marked as a dangerous subversive. You got 'em mad. And when you went into that teaching job and continued to rag on the big corps…No free pass, man."

Clay sipped his coffee, looking steely-eyed out over the ocean.

Eric was worried now. "Listen, Clay. I don't…"

"But, you know when I found out…" Clay took another sip and looked directly at Eric. "Well, let's just say I've got my own frustrations with the establishment and all its tentacles."

Eric was numb.

Clay calmly sipped his coffee. "Relax man. I'm not doin' you. I'm makin' my move to get out. But as you might imagine, you can't just quit the Company. It's like the Mafia. No one gets out alive. But I've got a plan that will save both our asses."

Eric collapsed back into the chair. "Wow. You waited 'til I was sober to tell me this, shit? Vicious... Man, I need a drink. Be right back." Eric pulled himself up and disappeared below.

Clay got up and looked around. No one in sight. Though the bright shiny day was becoming overcast.

Eric returned quickly with a bottle and offered to dump a bit in Clay's coffee mug. "Brandy... You puttin' me on with that CIA stuff? The CIA? Contract out on me?"

"Truth. Special Agent G. David Edwards directly assigned to your case. He was in the room with you and Dean Davis. Remember? Look man. It's real. Supposed to be surgical. Quick. In and out. You've got something they don't want out in the open. And they think it's in your head, so there's only one way to take care of that."

Eric was shaken, clutching the brandy bottle.

"Here's my ID." Clay took out his wallet and handed it to Eric.

Eric studied it. The ID card said it all. "Okay, okay. I believe you. But what I can't believe is that they want to kill me for bugging them about pollution. It's too much of a public issue. Everybody's talking about it."

"Like I said, they believe that you have confidential information that will hurt them."

"I do have information. Enough to bring down a certain oil company and prove collusion with the federal government... But that's just one company."

"You have provoked the wrong guys. They are very powerful and they want you dead. They gave you plenty of room. But, you got too much attention. Why run the risk that you might start a youth movement that might catch on? They can't publicly oppose you or attempt to take away your freedom of speech. That's bad form."

"Clay, you're starting to scare me."

"Do you remember the papers you copied when you worked at AP&G Oil?"

"How do you know about that?"

"It's my job, Eric. Do you recall a break-in at your house a few months ago? Police said it was a burglary, but just stupid stuff was missing. Remember?"

"Yeah, I remember?"

"Well, the CIA did the burglary and found the packet of information on AP&G Oil. They copied the files. But, like I said, you've got something they don't want out in the open. And they think it's in your head. So…there's only one way to take care of that."

"Clay, this is ridiculous…"

"It's the details, the facts in all those depositions and declarations attached in the thousands and thousands of motions in those files—facts no one is ever supposed to hear about…or put together."

"But I didn't read any of that. I didn't copy that. I only copied the allegations and judgments."

"Doesn't matter, man. You were there. You had access. They think you know it all. And that's more dangerous than some guy ramming a bunch of ships in international waters."

"This can't be happening…"

"I've known about the contract on you for a while. I had an assignment not long ago to go undercover, on the streets, look like a bum, fit in and tail a guy the Company wanted to bring in. This guy had dropped out of sight and was hiding as a homeless man. That's how I met Charlie and Bob. They are just bums. Hopeless drunks. Nobodies, really. I found my man and turned him over three days ago. That was when I was assigned my next job. A hit. An assassination. You."

"Whoa…" Eric backed away and grabbed the railing. He looked out at the empty ocean and then back at Clay.

"Early retirement, and a little accident. If you're murdered, you become a hero. If you just die quietly, well the public will always feel like you could have done so much more, if only you'd lived a little longer. Easiest method, Eric. You're out of the way and so is the issue. Believe me, it's done all the time. People are killed and the public is never the wiser. The Company has no morals. They just do as ordered, and they do it really well. They are lethal."

Clay took the bottle of brandy from Eric and poured a healthy measure in his coffee cup.

Eric didn't move.

"I had to think quickly. I called your house and Elaine told me you were going on this trip. So here we are: mid-ocean."

Eric turned back toward the water, gripping the rails with both hands, steadying himself.

Clay took a big gulp from his mug. "Eric, I plan to use Charlie and Bob to represent you and me. We'll have to disappear and start all over again. I'm putting the rest of it together as I go, but trust me, it'll work!"

"You mean to kill those two?"

"Yes."

"I don't want to be part of any murder, Clay. I had enough in 'Nam to last a…"

"Eric! You and I are dead men if we don't do this and these men are dead already. They've given up on themselves and society. Please, you must understand…"

"There must be some other way, Clay. I understand…

"Man, if you or I run they'll put us on their wanted list and they'll win in the long run."

"But murder… Clay, murder?"

"Man, you've got to get this straight. If I don't kill you, they'll kill me, and then they'll grab Elaine and find you and then they'll kill you both. You can't win. My way, you live. She lives. And the CIA is satisfied that you are dead. Case closed. Get it?"

Ten

A Dangerous Plan

Bob came topside, staggering up the stairs. Eric and Clay stopped talking.

"Say, Cap'n... And a good morning to you too, Clay. Say, do we have a little more of that snake that bit me? Sure could use a drink, Cap'n."

"Sure, sure. I'll get you another bottle, Bob."

As Eric left the deck he shouted over his shoulder. "Ok I'm in, Clay. I understand. I'm in."

Bob, still drunk, was quite oblivious to Eric's comment. "Thas the nizest man, Clay. Heee's a real genleman."

Clay smiled. "Drink it up, Bobby boy. There's lots more where that came from."

Eric returned from below and handed a fresh bottle to Bob.

Charlie was right behind him, a glass in his outstretched hand. "Good morning. Good morning. I'm gonna have a li'l breakfast myself, if you don't mind. Well, well, Bob, my friend. I think I'll try a bit from that new bottle."

Clay got up and went below. Eric and the two men sat silently watching the ocean as it gently rolled the ship. A beautiful morning, with distant clouds moving their way.

Eric broke the silence. "Well, it's time to weigh anchor, and get on our way. Can you guys give me a hand?"

"Sure, sure, Cap'n."

The three men set the sails and then Eric went to the wheelhouse and lifted the sea anchors. The ship started smoothly once again. Eric used the radio to get a weather report and was busy with the controls.

Clay returned from below decks and approached Bob and Charlie. "Look what I've got for you boys. As long as we're all pretending to be rich guys, a Rolex for you Charlie, and an Omega diver's chronometer for Bob. A nice school ring for you Charlie and a ring for you, Bob and a gold chain, too."

The two seemed reluctant at first

Clay spoke sincerely. "It's okay, guys. I asked Eric if we could wear the stuff. I told him it would make us feel good. We might just forget to return them when we get back, eh!" He winked at the two men.

"Clay boy, when you told us we were going on a great adventure, you really meant it didn't you. Jesus, all the booze you can drink, and gold and silver prizes, too! Look at us, Charlie!"

"Let's get some tunes going, man." The two sidled over to the other side of the boat, talking and drinking and playing the music very loud.

Eric and Clay decided to do a bit of fishing and talk some more.

Clay sat in the sea-chair and casted off. "All right, the stage is set. Charlie has my Rolex®, the number is registered to my name and my Harvard ring with an inscription inside. I gave Bob your chronometer, it has a registration number, too. Bob has your UC Berkeley ring and your wedding band."

Eric looked back at Bob and Charlie. "I don't see how this can work, Clay."

"Now look at those two idiots. Charlie is blond, with a little gray in his hair, my exact height and weight. Bob, dark graying hair and is a double for you. Is the plan becoming clear to you, yet?"

"I don't know, man."

"We'll let 'em get good and drunk, slide them over the side near the coastline and wait for the bodies to wash up on the shore."

Eric glared at Clay. "One error. Dental work. DNA. Yours and mine. It won't match. No, we got to think on this some more."

"Eric, it's a good plan. I know what they'll be looking for when they investigate. I didn't want to stress you about the dental work and DNA details, but we're committed now. So, here's the truth: we'll have to smash their faces in before they go over the side."

"You are truly a cruel bastard, Clay Perkins."

"Well it was your taxes that supported my education with the CIA, my boy. I wish I could say these were all my ideas, but the Company has been using them for many, many years and they got most of their ideas from the history books, pal.

"I-I…this is not my wheelhouse, Clay." Eric could feel his stomach wrenching.

"I'll take care of the gory details. That's my job. But I am gonna need your help."

As the beautiful day quickly waned and the dusk turned into a spectacular golden sunset, Bob and Charlie drank glass after glass of scotch whiskey. Just before nightfall they went below and passed out. They were dead drunk.

The sun was down and the wind picked up. The sea was becoming choppy as a storm brewed. Eric started the engines. The weather was getting pretty serious. Eric spent his time at the helm. Clay was beside him.

"Where the hell are we, Eric. How far from land?"

"Well, we should be… That is, if…"

"What's all this 'should be' and 'if' shit? Do you know—really know —where we are?"

"Hey, now the 'killer' is scared? Yes. I think I know where we are. But the only thing definite is that this storm is getting worse. We'll make it ol' buddy. Don't worry"

Eric turned on his electronic location instruments and pulled out his sextant and maps.

Before long, the growing wind caused the waves to slam into the vessel with great ferocity, delivering huge gushes of water over the sides of the ship.

Charlie and Bob came back up topside to see what all the noise was about. They were still drunk.

Eric and Clay were busy with the business of securing the ship during the storm. Eric called over. "Come on and help, you guys. We have to secure the canvas and rigging before the wind tears us apart."

Eric and Clay lowered the canvas, and without warning the boom broke loose from the mast, swinging menacingly to and fro. Eric called for all of the men to help him fasten the loosened piece. Just as they were about to get it tied down, the boat yawed. They lost their grip and the boom made one massive swing back hitting Bob in the face, knocking him against the rail.

Bob slid into a clump on the deck. Instantly, he was dead.

The remaining three fought to capture and steady the wildly moving boom and finally secured it. The storm showed no signs of lessening as the men took Bob's body below. They rolled him over and saw that his face was crushed, smashed beyond recognition.

Eric shouted. "My god, half of his head is gone. Oh shit, he's a mess."

Charlie, ever the practical one, stated the obvious. "Yeah. He's a bloody mess. And he's real dead. We all need a drink!"

The wind howled in a high-pitched scream. The storm continued tossing the ship about as the men eagerly wolfed down the whiskey and stared at the gory body of poor Bob.

Finally, Eric walked over to Clay and whispered. "Okay, quarterback. One down. Goal to go."

Clay stood up. "Well, nothing we can do for him. Let's go topside and make sure everything is secured."

Charlie shook his head. "I'm not going back up there. You can't make me do it. I need another drink, Clay."

Eric went to the liquor cabinet and got a fresh bottle for Charlie. He motioned to Clay to follow him and they both struggled up the steps to face the raging storm.

Topside, they labored to finish securing the boat against the heavy sheeting rain. Successful in their efforts, Clay and Eric took refuge from the storm in the little wheelhouse.

"What's our next move? What'll we do with Charlie?"

"I think we let him ride it out down there, Eric. Just him, and Bob. And the bottle. Say, how close are we to shore? Any idea in this storm?"

He smiled at Clay. "Still scared, Mr. Assassin? Not to worry. We should be less than a mile from the coast heading south along the Baja peninsula. We'll put in, if I can find that natural port; if it's on the charts. Clay, hold the wheel and let me look at this map again."

Eric peered through the window trying to look through the driving rain. "Well, I can see the Baja coast line out there, but until I take a reading, I won't be able to tell exactly where we are. I better put out a May Day call. This looks like it's gonna get rough."

Clay grabbed Eric's hand before it reached the radio. "No. No May Day. Don't want to alert anyone. We need time to be on our side."

Eric pulled back. "Okay, boss. I'll work on where we are. Give me a few minutes with the maps and the sextant. Why don't you go below and check on Charlie and get us a bottle of brandy. I'm freezing up here."

As the boat tossed and rolled, Eric tried to get a fix on their position. It was difficult. His mind was on Charlie. He wondered whether he could kill him in cold blood. Killing an enemy soldier in war, a person who was trying to kill you, was one thing. But premeditated murder?

His thoughts were interrupted as Clay climbed back into the wheelhouse.

Clay offered the brandy bottle to Eric. "Well, our passenger down there is guzzling the hooch like there's no tomorrow. And for him, there won't be."

Clay saw Eric's sullen expression. "Hey, you've got to get a handle on this thing, man. The Company is gonna kill you. There's a contract on you. This is war man. Bob and Charlie are the expendables. Remember how that works? Collateral damage. A KIA number."

Eric was listening, but changed the subject. "I think I've got a fix. If I'm right, we're close. It looks like we're less than a quarter of a mile from the coastline. The map shows a beach and a little cover, a good opening to get in. Once we get through, we'll have some refuge from this storm."

Eric grabbed the brandy and took a long pull on the bottle, wiped his mouth and handed it back. "Clay. Look, I know those guys have to be history. I can do it, but what then? What about my wife? What about Elaine? How do I get with her again and where will we live out the rest of our lives and what if..."

"Eric, Eric." Clay put his hands on Eric's shoulders. "Let's take one step at a time. You've got to get this boat out of the storm before we're torn to pieces. Then we'll talk. I promise you, there's usually an answer for every question. But not now. Let's focus on getting to land, first."

Eric guided the boat as best he could, but it was headed toward the rough coastal rocks. The entrance to the bay was a lot smaller than shown on the map and the bottom of the boat was scraping against the rocks.

A huge wave hit the starboard side of the boat. In one violent move, the boat was slammed into the jagged rocks.

Water poured into the boat, flooding the area below decks. Eric tried to move the boat off the rocks, but it was stuck tight.

Clay looked at Eric went below. Eric followed.

Charlie had been thrown against the wall. He was breathing, but his neck was obviously broken.

Clay pulled loose a table leg and hit Charlie's head and mouth again and again until there was no face, just a crushed skull and a gaping hole without a nose or teeth.

Eric leaned against the ladder, watching.

Then with greater force, Clay bashed Bob's head to a similar condition. Both dead men were now unrecognizable.

Clay turned to Eric. "Come on man. Now's the time."

Eric and Clay dragged Bob's body topside and dumped him over the side and then went below to get Charlie. They struggled. It took tremendous effort from both of them to pull the heavier Charlie up to the deck and then throw him off into to the raging waters.

It was done.

Without warning, the boat then lurched off the rocks and toward the shore. Eric and Clay held on for their lives. The wave took the boat within a hundred feet of the shore and abruptly flipped it over.

Clay and Eric jumped away into the turbulent waters. They both swam for the shore as the violent seas lashed about them.

As they looked back, the boat crashed and splintered into pieces.

Eleven

Playing Dead

Exhausted and cold, they laid on the beach for some time as the storm raged on. Then, as happens with tropical storms, it suddenly quit and the air became warmer.

They were wet and bruised, but alive. Eric looked at Clay. "God damn, that was one hell of a ride!"

They sat watching the nearly calm waves depositing pieces of the boat on the shore. Suddenly, one of the dead bodies washed ashore. Clay went over and pulled it further up onto the beach.

Before long the other body popped up twenty yards to the south and the waves gently threw it on the shore. Clay pulled that body up on the sand.

Little crabs had emerged and were beginning to eat the first body. Clay went over and scooped up a few and took them to the other body. Soon, hundreds of crabs were busily eating the cadavers. Now the feast was joined by the sea gulls.

Eric was sick and vomited. He had swallowed a lot of seawater. Or maybe it was the sight of those horribly mutilated bodies being devoured by the feral creatures.

Clay stood over Eric and patted him on the back. "Let's get off this beach."

Away from the water and the mutilation, they climbed up a low hill. Upon reaching the top, they saw a small village not more than quarter of a mile away.

Eric pointed, "Civilization, such as it is."

Excitedly Clay said, "Okay. I've got the plan now. Eric, have you got your wallet?"

"Well, yes. Guess we forgot to put it on the boys."

Clay reached into his own pocket and pulled out a wallet. "We sure did. I've still got mine, too. Let's go back down the hill and put them on the bodies."

They scrambled down the hill and approached the dead men. Both stood in amazement at the efficiency of nature. Even though much of the flesh was being neatly removed from the bodies, it wasn't easy to distinguish who was who except that their clothing was different. The clothes were remarkably intact.

"Leave the money in the wallets." Clay ordered. "I've got plenty more in my belt."

They quickly slipped the wallets into the respective pockets of the dead men and silently continued to watch the crabs and birds at their work.

Eric spoke. "So, what's this bright idea you've had?"

"Right. Right. Okay, try this on. I'll do it by the numbers. Bodies are found. Got ID on them and distinguishing features: height, build, hair color. Right? They have wallets, rings, watches, gold chain, etc. So..."

"God. I forgot that I told Elaine I would call her every third day. This is day three."

"Don't worry. Elaine will report that she hasn't heard from you. I'm sure the Company will pick up on it. Maybe the media, too. The storm is a matter of fact that will be entered on the metrological logs, and with all of that confusion, it gains us some time. But, in fact, there's no time to waste. Back to what we're going to do. Here's the plan."

Clay stood up and started pacing as he continued. "Bodies are taken to the nearest *estación de policía*. I appear with my cover FBI ID and tell the cop that because they are obviously Americans the FBI will want pictures, fingerprints, coroner's report, police report, the works. I pay the cop some cash, and more cash to the coroner if necessary. I tell the cop to hold all the details, to put a lid on this case and to tell no one and make no reports of any kind until I give him the go-ahead."

"What about the DNA?"

"We spill our own blood on the clothing, urinate and defecate on the clothes soak them in sea water and leave them behind bundled in a bag. That'll give the CIA investigators plenty of DNA."

"Wait. I'm confused. FBI is domestic. CIA is international, right? So, why is an FBI agent negotiating with foreign police? Do you have the cop call in the Feds—the FBI? Do you have the cop order the coroner to have the bodies disposed of and give them more cash, more persuasion..."

"Almost right, Eric. Remember, it's the CIA who has the contract. They are the ones who'll need convincing. So the FBI will eventually become a tool to convince the Company. I'll have the cop make up the final report as I dictate it. That way it'll be done right."

"Okay, but how do you get the coroner and the cops to do all this and keep it secret when the feds arrive? The CIA or FBI or whatever?"

"First, money buys just about anything. Cooperation for cash, and then, well dead men tell no tales."

"Jesus, Clay. Murder again? The cop and the coroner? This is getting out of hand."

"Stand-by pal. It'll probably get a lot messier. You gotta trust me. Now let's go into town and do a little reconnaissance."

They crawled back up the hill from the beach and walked toward a little Mexican village. After arriving, they surveyed the scene and Clay asked a local where *la policía*, could be found.

Eric was amazed at how fluent Clay was with the local Mexican dialect and how quickly he got directions to the house of the local policeman. They trudged on.

Once inside, Clay introduced himself and got on with the Mexican official with no hitches and no questions. The cop was just finishing a glass of tequila and opened another bottle and offered them a drink. He introduced himself as Chief of Police, Armando Ruiz.

Clay knew what he was doing. He showed the cop his identification and explained that they were with the FBI and on a very secret and covert mission. He told Chief Ruiz that they had just endured a shipwreck and that they needed the Chief's help. And that there were two men dead on the beach.

Clay spun a tale of how the men had been killed in the boat wreck and that if this information became public, it would result in great problems for Mexico. He explained that he needed a truck to pick up the bodies from the beach and then the coroner should do an autopsy. He cautioned that no one but Chief Ruiz and the coroner must know of this.

Clay turned to Eric who was just catching on to the plan. He whispered. "Eric and Clay are dead. Got it? We'll work out the details for the future when we get out of this mess."

Clay gave Chief Ruiz two one hundred dollar bills for expenses and promised him more. He told the policeman that they would need some sheets to wrap up the bodies and a large bucket.

Chief Ruiz only asked once what it was all about. Clay assured him that he would explain everything and that he would assist in making a detailed report. And, if he did everything right, Chief Ruiz would be greatly rewarded. Clay asked Chief Ruiz if he had a camera. The Chief answered that he had a Polaroid and some film.

All was well. Clay was very good at his trade.

Chief Ruiz offered the use of his personal truck. He took a long pull on his bottle of tequila and then ushered them all into his old Ford pickup truck parked in front.

They drove off toward the bay. Soon, they moved through a little opening in the hills and drove down the beach to where the bodies lay waiting. The crabs and birds had done even more damage.

Clay instructed Ruiz to take pictures of the bodies lying on the beach. Chief Ruiz began drinking very seriously after seeing the dead men.

The sun was just setting as they wrapped the bodies and loaded them into the pick-up truck. Clay dipped the bucket into the surf filling it with seawater. Clay asked Ruiz to take them to the coroner's office.

Chief Ruiz reminded Clay that this was a small village. The coroner was also the town's doctor, dentist and the funeral director, and he worked out of his own home.

Clay shot a look at Eric.

Chief Ruiz ushered them back into the truck. They made their way to the coroner's house.

They unloaded their grisly cargo in the back room, where the dead were normally prepared. One of the bodies was lifted up on a crude wooden drain table. The conditions were quite primitive but more than adequate for what Clay needed them to do.

The coroner, Dr. Gutierrez, was not well versed in modern police forensics. He lacked the skill and scientific equipment to do a proper autopsy, though he was quite familiar with how to dispose of the dead.

Chief Ruiz introduced Clay as a man who was with the FBI and an expert. The doctor followed all of Clay's instructions without objection.

Clay reinforced the importance of doing a thorough job. He outlined for the doctor and Chief of Police what needed to be included in the reports. Clay had Ruiz write each step on the back of large brown evidence envelopes. First, the bodies were photographed and their date of discovery printed on the evidence envelopes and noted in the police and coroner's reports.

Chief Ruiz asked Dr. Gutierrez for tequila. With this new bottle passed around to all, the repulsive job of examining the two cadavers became a bit more agreeable. Clay again stressed that all of this was of national importance for both of their countries. He concluded his speech with more hundred dollar bills. With the cash in their hands, they agreed and eagerly followed directions.

The next procedure was to itemize the personal effects. The wallets, the rings, the gold chains and the watches were all put on the counter, photographed, and neatly listed on the backs of the big envelopes. Clay made sure that Eric's and his own real fingerprints were on each item.

Then the clothes were removed from each of the dead bodies. Clay interrupted and asked whether he and his "associate" could get some dry clothes to change into. The doctor provided them with hats, clothes and shoes locals had abandoned related to his funeral operation, and showed the two men into another room where they could change.

While the examiners were busy, Clay stealthily used a scalpel on Eric and himself cutting a small area on their arms until they got quite a bit of blood from each. With a rag, Clay painted the blood onto their clothing. They both urinated and defecated in their underwear and then stripped. Clay dipped the rubber gloves the doctor had given he and Eric into the bucket of sea water, filling them about a third of the way. The urine soaked underwear, their clothing and shoes and socks were mixed with the remaining seawater and packed in plastic garbage bags that Clay marked appropriately with their names. This would hopefully give the bodies a DNA match.

Eric and Clay were naked. Quickly, they changed into the native clothes the doctor had provided. Complete with hats and suntanned skin they began to look like locals.

Eric and Clay rejoined the doctor and Chief Ruiz and assisted in loading the removed clothing into bags. Clay deftly switched the bags of their clothes for the bags of the dead men's clothes.

Photos of the corpses were again taken again by Chief Ruiz with his ancient Polaroid, as Doctor Gutierrez presented first one body, and then the other.

Eric and Clay put on the rubber gloves filled with seawater and kept them on until their fingers were very wrinkled, as though they had be in the water, while the doctor recited his findings and Chief Ruiz recorded them in the reports.

Now it was time for the fingerprints. Clay "helped" with collecting the prints from each cadaver as the doctor made notes on his report and Chief Ruiz added to his. The print cards would show Eric and Clay's fingerprints, shriveled and loaded with ocean water. With the presentation of more money and assurance that they would be well taken care of, Chief Ruiz and Dr. Gutierrez dutifully signed their name on each card below the prints and put them in the envelopes.

The doctor drafted the conclusion to his report. He stated that he was convinced that both men had died from injuries in the boat wreck and drowning. Their bodies had been devastated by trauma, birds and marine creatures.

Dr. Gutierrez and Chief Ruiz then wrapped the bodies neatly in sheets and tied them up securely.

Clay checked all of the evidence over and over again until he was completely satisfied.

Clay again stressed to the officials that this was to be kept quiet. Clay showed them a wad of hundred dollar bills and promised them as soon as this was all done, they would get even more as their reward. Both men seemed happy and eagerly agreed to remain silent.

About 9:00 p.m., Clay instructed Chief Ruiz to make a call to the police department in San Diego and report the deaths. Chief Ruiz was only to mention the dead men's names. He was not to reveal that the "FBI agents" had been present or participated in any way. He was to limit discussion only to the two dead men.

Clay listened as Chief Ruiz spoke exactly as ordered.

Ruiz told the homicide detective in San Diego the dead men's names. "*Si, señor*, identification found on the bodies shows they are Clay B. Perkins and Eric T. Atkinson... *Si, señor*, I have both driver's license cards."

Chief Ruiz read the driver's license numbers and recited other vital statistics. He told the San Diego detective that he and the coroner had made full reports, including photographs, inventory of personal effects and fingerprints. He added that they had bagged the clothes and personal effects. The detective told Chief Ruiz that the San Diego police would act on it immediately.

Clay knew when the San Diego police contacted the FBI, they'd contact the CIA, since this was an international incident. When Clay's name was mentioned he knew investigators from the Company would leave as soon as they could to confirm that Clay had completed the job he'd agreed to do. Clay expected they would probably be there by the next morning.

Chief Ruiz hung up the phone.

Dr. Gutierrez asked when the Americans would come for the bodies.

Clay and Eric looked at one another. Clay asked what the detective had said.

Chief Ruiz reported that the detective did not mention anything about retrieving the bodies.

Dr. Gutierrez reminded Chief Ruiz that they had no refrigeration and it was not possible to bury the bodies. The vermin that had attacked the bodies on the beach were becoming an issue. Dr. Gutierrez reminded them all that this was his home, after all.

Clay smiled broadly, helpfully and told Chief Ruiz that they had the reports and they'd bagged all of the personal effects and clothing. He instructed Chief Ruiz to add a final note in his report. "The bodies are rapidly decomposing. Since we have no refrigeration here, and these bodies cannot be buried in the hallowed ground of our cemetery, Dr. Gutierrez and I have decided to bury them at sea."

Chief Ruiz and Dr. Gutierrez looked knowingly at one another. Things were suddenly becoming clearer.

Clay put more money on the table.

Chief Ruiz added the few sentences to his report and Dr. Gutierrez signed off.

Clay asked if there was a rowboat nearby. Ruiz answered yes. Clay told the doctor and the chief of police that if they would help them get the bodies into the sea before sunrise, they'd be handsomely rewarded. The two nodded in agreement.

Clay ordered Ruiz to gas up his truck at the cantina and tell them that he and Dr. Gutierrez were going out of town on business, but they would be back by tomorrow morning.

The doctor and police chief loaded the sheet-wrapped bodies into the pick-up truck. Clay and Eric got in the back of the truck with the dead men.

They traveled about a half-mile south. The road curved down toward the ocean.

In a silent cove, the four men filled the sheet around each wrapped body with stones, retied them and hauled the grisly packages to a row-boat and loaded the bodies inside. With the moon giving them plenty of light, they rowed out into the open water.

About a half mile out, where the water was very deep, they slipped the dead bodies overboard.

The silent thoughts of the four men were the only memorial service that poor Charlie and Bob were to receive.

It was though none of this had ever happened.

Silently, they rowed back to the shore and all four of them got into the pick-up truck.

Clay sat up front so he could talk to the Chief Ruiz. "Take us on to La Paz, Chief. We'll get a plane out of there and I'll give you and Dr. Gutierrez the money I promised. You've done a good job, *amigo*. You've earned your reward."

The truck headed east on a dirt road. Once they were on Baja High-way 1, a macadam road, they traveled southeast.

Just about fifteen miles outside of La Paz, Clay motioned to Ruiz to pull over. They all got out of the truck and each one began to take a piss.

Suddenly, with lighting speed, Clay hit Chief Ruiz and Dr. Gutierrez, knocking them both unconscious.

Eric watched in awe. "What now?"

"Well, here's the story. These two guys were attacked by *banditos*. They were beaten, robbed and left on the side of the road and their truck was stolen. That's my story. Now here's the action."

From the back of the truck Clay took a tire-iron and beat the two men to death. Then he took their wallets and the money he had given them, their watches and rings, and motioned Eric back into the truck.

They left the beaten, bloodied bodies and traveled slowly down the road in the pick-up truck toward La Paz.

Eric was trying to process everything. "Okay. I've helped to kill four people, been in a shipwreck, broken God knows how many laws, domestic and international and I'm a dead man. I no longer exist. This is real. So, what do we do now, ol' buddy?"

Twelve

A New Life

Clay mumbled. "New life. Old dreams. Something useful. All that's true. Hell if I know, Eric. Yeah. We're dead to the world. But you're still alive, and so am I. Beats having the 'man' killing us for real, doesn't it?"

"Yeah, I guess it does. I guess I owe you my life, again, don't I?"

"Don't worry. I'm not going to call-in that favor just yet."

A battered sign on Baja Highway 1 told them that La Paz was only 9 miles ahead.

"All right. La Paz to where?"

"Mazatlan."

"Okay. Clay, I want to stop a while and think about this new life. I need to figure out what to do."

"You said a lot of shit on the boat about how the government is allowing big corporations to poison the environment just to make the fat cats, fatter. You said the pollution is quickly reaching the point of no return that it must be stopped. I asked you what you would do to bring it to an end, if you could. Did you mean all that?"

"That's why I want to stop for a minute, Clay. Think of what I can do, and make a plan. I've got a sketchy idea happening in my brain right now. I want to get it organized, try it on you and see what you think."

Clay nodded in agreement.

Eric changed the subject. "Clay, you know how this FBI-CIA thing works. What will they do? Do you think any of that really fooled them? Will we get away with it or will there be two contracts to kill, now?"

"Depends on who gets the case. If it becomes a routine investigation, and they buy that we're dead, no problem. I did my job in service of my country, as agreed and done deal. If it lights a fire under someone's ass, and they pursue us until they find out the details... Well, I just hope Agent Dave Edwards is convinced. He's one tough son-of-a-bitch. But don't worry. I think we did a pretty good job of throwing them off. We'll know soon enough."

"Clay, I know you know what you're doing, but are we going to drive right into the airport with this truck?"

"Oh, no Watson. We're going to ditch this truck in the city. With the Mexican *Policía Federal* now a fully-funded faction of the US Justice Department, they'll put out an APB on this old truck for sure. We'll lose the truck in population and take some public transportation to the airport. We're dressed in local style, so we should blend in with the natives. Then I think we'll go to the sunny beaches of Mazatlan and let you develop our new life plan and just hang out for a few days, while I try to tap in and find out exactly what our federal hound dogs are up to."

As the truck entered the city limits of La Paz, for the first time in months, Eric had a sense that his new future would be brighter than his past. He squashed the remorse he felt about the killings and the ache he felt missing Elaine with his emerging understanding that he was going to finally do something that would make a positive difference in the world. That made it all worth it.

They left the truck, and walked to La Paz airport. At the ticket counter Clay bought the tickets for Mazatlan with Mexican currency.

They left the counter and went to a little cantina-style bar and ordered two *cervezas*.

"Okay, Clay, I'm not too smart about these spy-things, but how'd you get that much local cash? Was it smart to use that to buy the tickets?".

"Listen, bud. I know what I'm doing. We'll talk about it when we hit the beach at Mazatlan. Got it?"

CIA Agent G. David Edwards landed in Puerto Vallarta and then made his way north to the little village to start his investigation. Edwards had to beg his superiors to go on this trip. They said he had better things to do. He convinced them that Clay Perkins was a clever man and wanted to absolutely confirm that Atkins and Perkins were dead.

Edwards discovered rapidly that there were an awful lot of odd holes in this case, not the least of which were the fact that the chief of police and the doctor on the case were found dead. Edwards called back to Los Angeles and ordered a forensic team to come down to Mexico.

Agent Edwards was thinking. "Got to make sure that it was Clay and Eric. No bodies. Everything is too pat. All in order, not like the sloppy work usually done by the Mexicans. All their effects in envelopes, finger prints, etc. Am I being a little paranoid? It could be just as it seems, that they are both dead. Well, the forensic boys will sort it out."

The flight for Clay and Eric was a short one. In less than one hour they arrived in Mazatlan.

Clay wanted to keep a low profile. They required some better clothes and shoes. They shopped at three different stores so as not to arouse suspicion, and stopped at a pharmacy to purchase some toiletries. They found a decent inexpensive tourist hotel near the beach and checked in.

In order to color his blond hair brown, Clay purchased some hair and beard dye. Clay called out to Eric from the bathroom. "Time to let that beard and mustache come back, old man."

Eric was beginning to enjoy this spy-movie adventure.

Back in the little Mexican village, the CIA supervised the FBI forensic team, who took clothing samples stained with the blood and feces from the labeled bag of soiled clothes for DNA testing. Both of the dead men had their DNA on file with the FBI. The chief forensic man told

Agent Edwards that it could take a week to get a match, or even a divergent conclusion.

David Edwards did not like the delay, but understood that it would take some time to get the lab results.

The CIA agents and the FBI forensic team packed their samples and loaded them into the van that would take them to Puerto Vallarta to catch a plane back to the U.S.

After a good night's rest, Eric and Clay headed down to the beach in Mazatlan. The two entered the Gulf of California for a long and satisfying swim. The water was surprisingly warm and the weather balmy.

After their swim, they lay on the beach towels and were warmed by the sun.

Eric was the first to speak. "Clay, I think I have a plan. I've thought about it for years. Now maybe it's time to stop talking and get on with it. *Acta non verba*, as they say."

Clay, eyes closed, didn't move, soaking up the warm rays of the sun. "Okay. I'm listening."

Eric got up on one elbow. "The environment is really messed up. Natural disasters, man slowly disrupting nature, poisoning himself, destroying the world and its future generations. Animals half-dead, or dead before they are slaughtered and sent to market, animals that are filled with pesticides and antibiotics which are killing and maiming people and causing a wide-spread immune deficiency in the whole population. The government's denial that we are the largest emitter of CO^2 greenhouse gases in the entire world, the absolute refusal to use alternative energy sources to clean up our rampant and ever-growing air pollution because big money and oil control our government. And then, the phony politics and false statements of clean-up..."

Clay was listening. "That clean-up'll never happen, man. It's all a game."

Eric sat up. "But, these violators have to be stopped–cold. I know the technical and legal issues will always be up for debate. That's someone else's problem, like the EPA, FDA, the environmental lawyers. I believe now that force is the only answer."

Clay was up on one elbow now. "You know about Agent Orange, right? What it did to us?

Eric looked down. "Yeah. Thanks, Dow-Monsanto. Some defoliant. Pretty sure the Agent Orange in my system caused Elaine to miscarry—twice. The government knew and didn't care. Dow and Monsanto—they're just whores for hire."

Clay sat up, too. "Sorry, man."

Eric was getting angry. "It just doesn't stop. Here at home, our poor management of city garbage in landfills, methane build-up. And the run-off from chicken, pig, beef farming ruining the surrounding aquifers. Petrochemical companies—the biggest criminals of pollution. Three Mile Island...nuclear energy producers are polluters, too, you know. Our water, our air, the food we eat... It's all being poisoned just so the big corporations can make more profits.

Clay looked at Eric and dropped back on one elbow. "But, today, you couldn't get the big corporations to stop polluting even if you used a cannon. They just won't..."

Eric sat bolt upright. "That's it! Don't you see? They won't stop, so we have to *stop them*. *We* stop them!"

Clay sat up again. "We? Stop them? How? Guns? Bombs? Fighting? Eric, I assure you, that's a bad idea. I think it was Sun Tzu who said 'Never underestimate your enemy.' You can't go up against the system. It's too big. You can't win. They're too powerful. We can't fight the entire U.S. military..."

"Oh, yes we can. The 'how to do it' synapses are going wild in my brain right now. All we need is some funding, some trained military guys on our side, access to weaponry, and..."

"Whoa. Whoa. You just said a mouthful, Eric. A lot of money, experienced men, and weapons. You need all that. And, look around pal...We don't have it. You're nuts, Eric. It can't be done."

"I have to try, Clay. I can't keep just talking about this. When you can actually see the existing pools of toxins and the poisonous run-offs into the aquifers, the lakes and streams and rivers that are so loaded with petrol on top of them, that you can set them on fire. If there's a way… Imagine, if we could do it, we could make a real change. The world might once again become healthy and safe."

They both lay back on the towels and stopped talking.

After a while, Clay got up and stood over Eric. "You know, we're doing this all wrong. We're supposed to work in the morning, eat a nice lunch and then have our *siesta*. I'm getting hungry. Let's eat."

Eric agreed with him and they headed for the hotel to change for lunch.

They wandered around the streets of Mazatlan until they found an interesting place. Strangely the sign in the window said: *Joe's Diner*.

Inside, it looked clean enough. The menu offered some fascinating items:

Corned beef hash with mole sauce and corn chips

Joe's own beef bocadillo with salsa verde

Chicago Style Mexican Chili

Southern Fried Pollo with mashed papa

Vienna Hot Dog in a soft tortilla.

The menu offered real Coca-Cola® in bottles. From the menu, they suspected that the owner was a Mexican-American ex-patriot named José, from Chicago, no doubt.

Clay ordered in Spanish for both of them. Eric sat mute and just nodded and ate the food that was delivered.

During the lunch neither of them spoke much. As Clay paid the bill, he said to Eric. "You know, I've been thinking about what you said on the beach this morning. I'm going to make a phone call to a man who might want to get involved. You probably don't remember him. He was in 'Nam with us. Billy Johnstone."

"Yes," said Eric. "I remember him. We had many conversations about the way things are in this world, as opposed to how we thought they should be. He was against any kind of war. He thought we should have learned enough not to make war. I remember he said that mankind seems to repeat its mistakes. He was committed to doing something to change the world. Billy was smart. He had some interesting ideas, but he seemed pretty straight-laced. Why do you think he would want to get involved?"

"Well, to begin with, Billy is now a multi-billionaire and a big advocate for social and ecological change. Just a hunch. I'll call him tonight and see if he'll meet with us."

They left *Joe's* and found a *cantina*. It was *cerveza* time!

Thirteen

Hot on Their Trail

In Los Angeles, CIA Agent David Edwards received a call from his direct superior in Washington, DC.

"Edwards, I have your report on Eric Atkins and our agent Clay Perkins. I see that you have ordered a complete DNA test of the samples taken from the bodies in Mexico. What's your assessment at this time?"

"I know we have all of the *prima facie* evidence to say that both dead men are Atkins and Perkins, but somehow I have a hunch that things are not as they seem. Even though the prints belong to these guys, we've got no fingers on the bodies to match to them—'cause there are no bodies. We do have some blood and urine and hair samples that are being tested. But there are other things that bother me. The medical report was quite thorough, not the kind done in a small Mexican village. And, the doctor who did the autopsy and the chief of police have been murdered. Allegedly a robbery gone bad. It's a real mystery. I'll wait for the tests to come back and get a few more details resolved before I close this one, boss."

"David, I've read the file. The evidence is very solid. The facts, as they stand, substantiate that Atkins and Perkins are dead. Perkins seems to have completed his assignment as agreed. And, in reality, that cleans up a lot of loose ends about Atkins and Perkins, doesn't it? I want a final report so we can close this matter, ASAP. In the meantime, get off this one and onto another case, and that's an order."

Edwards heard the order loud and clear, but in the back of his mind he still wanted to wait for the DNA reports and put together a few more details. His boss would have to wait a little while longer for a final report on this case.

At the *cantina* in Mazatlan, after a couple of bottles of the good local *cerveza*, Clay got up and wandered off.

In about fifteen minutes he returned. "Your flamin' rivers gave me an idea."

Eric looked puzzled. "What?"

Clay sat back down. "Talked with Billy. He'll see us tomorrow afternoon at *Joe's Diner*. He knows the place. I told him it would be a good spot to meet."

Eric was astounded. "You sure know how to make it happen, *kemosabe*. I'm impressed. So, I guess Billy lives here in Mazatlan?"

"No, he'll fly in from the Gulf Coast on his private jet."

"Right. Of course. What did you say to him to get him to move so quickly? Did you tell him the end of the world is near?"

"Just reminded him of *semper fi*. Told him I needed a little conversation and some serious help. Over the years I've been in touch with Billy, and his right-hand man, Rob Collings. I've done them both favors here and there. You remember Collings, don't you? It was Captain Collings back then."

"Yes, I do. A real hard-ass gyrene if ever there was one!"

"Yeah, he was all by-the-book. Listen, Eric. This is it. Between now and tomorrow you need to come up with a convincing presentation for them. Of course, if Billy doesn't buy it, we'll still get a ride back to the good ol' U.S. of A."

Eric went out of the hotel and straight to the *farmacia* where he bought a legal pad, folders and various pens.

Back in his room, Eric began to map out his plan.

"What is the strategy? What targets should be considered? What is the time frame? What specialists will be needed? What equipment? What transportation? What weaponry? Supplies?..." He said it all out loud as though someone was listening.

"How the hell do I know?" He argued with himself aloud. "If Billy is interested, all that can be put together. I don't want to get lost in the details. What I need is an easy to understand concept and general strategy."

Eric wrote feverishly, listing only the high points of his plan in a rough bullet-style presentation.

The next morning, Eric and Clay showered, shaved and had their coffee. They were ready to meet with Billy.

About 10:00 a.m., there was a knock on the hotel room door.

It was Billy Johnstone and Rob Collings.

Billy burst into the room and shook Clay's hand firmly. "Hey, Clay. Good seeing you again. What the hell are you up to and what kind of trouble are you in?"

"Good to see you, Billy. And you too, Rob. Yeah, we're in a world of shit, guys. By the way, this is Eric Atkins. I don't know if you remember him, Billy. It's been a long time since we've all been together. Too many years, now."

"I sure do remember, Eric." Billy grasped Eric's hand and squeezed it firmly. "How're you doing, man? Those talks you and I had when the bullets weren't flyin' are stuck in my memory. Remember you? Hell, I want to thank you. Truth be known, Eric, you probably inspired me to take the path in life that I've taken. Biotechnology, WFJ Biotechnology, that is. Good seein' you again, buddy. What have you done since 'Nam, Eric?"

"Big compliments, Billy. Thank you. Well, for many years now I've tried to be on both sides of the fence. Teaching biology and ecology and speaking out against the horrible pollution that's hurting our environment. I had a pretty good teaching job at Hardeston Institute, but blew that one with my big mouth. That university is almost entirely funded by big oil, petrochemical and pharmaceutical companies. They went to 'uncle' with my noise, and 'uncle' decided I should be dead. Clay here was CIA and got the lucky draw to take me out. Instead, he put together a brilliant plan for us to disappear. Billy, I've been a pain in the ass to many major corporations, and very critical of the EPA's lack of responsibility to the people. I might add that your WFJ Corporation is a model that other businesses should follow. As far as I have learned, you don't pollute and you have personally made it a company policy that you will not tolerate any pollution."

"Yes, Eric. That is our guiding principle—do no harm. Thought it out from the beginning and we've adhered to that very idea. Now it's company law. No pollution. And if there is an accident, we clean it up immediately. No EPA citations for WFJ."

Clay interrupted. "Billy, I don't want to get in the middle of this mutual admiration, but Eric and I have a plan to do something. It's a bit radical. But, it might put a dent in this major corporate pollution. Maybe stop it forever."

"That's big talk, but I'm all ears, Clay."

"Well, it's Eric's concept, so I'll let him tell you about it. Have a seat, guys."

The four moved to a table in the center of the room and sat down.

Eric remained standing. "Okay, here's the deal, Billy. As you know, corporations are ruining the air, the water, the oceans, our food chain and causing global warming. The government, the EPA and FDA are supposed to keep them honest, but they don't. They levy fines, the big corps pay the fines and after they pay, it's business as usual. These greedy corporations realize that paying the fines is cheaper than cleaning up the pollution they have caused, and cheaper yet than employing manufacturing methods that don't pollute. In the last hundred years there have been more poisons added to our environment than in all previously recorded history. With the years of accumulation, these toxins have become a huge threat to humanity and its future. It's not just in the United States, it's worldwide…"

Billy interrupted. "Let me stop you there. I agree with everything you've said, Eric. But what is your plan and how do I fit in?"

"Yeah, I guess I'm doing a lecture here and singing to the choir and you know all the tunes. Okay, Billy. Here's what I want to do. If the EPA and the FDA can't, or won't, stop these violators, we will. I want to use force to destroy their property, hit them where they live. Money. With media coverage and real financial losses, I think we can put a stop to these unchecked polluters, and educate the public so that the people will never let it happen again."

"So, you want to blow up the plants that are guilty of polluting. Is that where you're going with this?" Billy looked at Rob, and then back at Eric and Clay.

With great sobriety, Eric and Clay nodded in agreement.

"And, you want me to provide the resources—labor, money, materiel?

Eric and Clay again nodded yes.

"You know you're playin' with fire, boys. You'll probably get hurt. And in the end, it may not make a difference."

Eric and Clay were like double bobble-heads as they again confirmed their agreement to Billy's comments.

"Eric you're married, aren't you? And Clay, you've got a great career in the CIA. That's a lot to risk, boys."

Clay spoke. "Well, here's the deal, Billy. We're dead men. As Eric told you, I got a CIA assignment to kill him because some influential guys didn't like his activism and certain information he possessed. I agreed to a suicide mission. I decided, for old times and *semper fi*, not to do him. I wanted out of the Company, anyway. I set up a scenario so it looked like we both died in a boat wreck off Baja. We called you after we covered our tracks. That ruse should hold up for a while, maybe forever. But CIA agent, G. David Edwards is investigating. He never liked me much. He's a hound-dog on Eric's tail. And, he's no fool."

Eric continued. "But that's a concern for tomorrow, because we're dead men now. We have nothing to lose by trying this. And, we just might pull it off!"

Eric sat down and looked directly at Billy. "So, now you know everything, Billy. What do you think? Will you help us?"

Billy got up and paced the room. "My gut says you just might get away with it and do some good. But, my good sense says it's a fool's errand. I got plenty of money so that's not a consideration. It's an exciting idea. And, I think it's high time somebody did something instead of playing the old political game and just talking about it. But..." Billy trailed off, pivoted and looked at the group in silence for a moment.

Eric's face fell. He didn't have any other ideas. He looked at Clay, who stared blankly out the window.

After an uncomfortable silence, Billy sat back down and slapped the table hard, garnering everyone's attention. "So. Yes, dammit. I'm in. And so is Rob Collings and all the resources of WFJ. First, the four of us will make proper plans to ensure success, and then... Hell, yes. It's a go!"

They all shouted. *"Semper fi! Hoo-rah."*

After an excellent Mexican dinner, they each got a bottle of tequila and some *cerveza* and headed back to the hotel.

Billy plopped down in a chair and flatly asked. "So what's your idea of a strategy, boys."

Clay spoke first. "My thinking is we form a small group of specialists: ForceRecon, Rangers, NavySeals. It'll be guerrilla warfare using military special forces tactics. Hit and run."

Eric passed out some hand-written pages he'd copied at the hotel desk. "Okay, here are the big points. First: the targets. I think that we should do some research and target the largest and most habitual EPA violators: the powerful oil companies and their oil and petrochemical refineries and off-shore drilling operations. Then the electric power stations, who are the biggest coal burners. These are the companies that are polluting our air and water and emit as much SO_2 and CO_2 as all of the gas and diesel engines. Then to the food chain. Those that have been cited by the FDA as flagrant violators: the factory farms, feedlots, slaughter and packing houses, and the food manufacturers. Then the big chemical producers, as well as several of the big pharmaceutical companies."

Eric took a breath. "Believe me, there is a long list. In fact, the problems are so huge and the violators are so many that it would take a lifetime to damage all of them completely."

Billy interrupted him. "No, we do not want all of them. What we need to do is to pick off the biggies, the ones that will squeal the loudest, and will get the media and the public's attention. That's how you make 'em lose money."

Eric nodded his approval. "Now, I'll move on to the strategy; Clay's idea of hit and run. Gulf Coast one day, West Coast two days later, Chicago in two days, New Jersey, then East Coast, then into Washington state. It'll drive them crazy trying to figure out where we are and what we'll do next. And if we can ensure that our explosives and equipment are in place in advance and our team is undetectable, we'll be invincible!"

Billy interrupted. "Okay so far, Eric. Rob, can we deliver the stuff they'll need for their operations?"

Billy and Rob Collings had been to war. A trained officer, Collings understood exactly what was needed and how to deploy and employ it.

Collings considered for a moment: "We can get plenty of what they need and we can discreetly distribute it in advance to their selected locations. It shouldn't be a problem. Yeah, we can do it."

Eric was thrilled. "All right! Number three: the tactics. Okay, I need input here. The problem is, in putting these plants out of business, we don't want to cause more pollution. If we just take out the offices and computers, they can still manufacture. It's probably a combination of destroying computers and security systems, contamination of the product if possible, and irreparable damage to processing equipment. What do you guys think?"

Clay jumped in. "Each one of those issues requires a different approach and some of them have an inherent danger of exposure to us with the possibility of capture, injury, or death. I vote to blow 'em and go."

Collings nodded his head in agreement. "Yeah. If you're gonna make your point, do damage and get the hell out."

Billy weighed in last. "I think each one is a judgment call. If you just want to cripple them, do so. If you want to level the entire operation, do it. If a company's operation needs to be stopped then it should be stopped. It'll be your call at the planning stage, Eric. You'll be responsible for the research and recon for planning. You know the details on these companies. I think with a little more research and recon you'll know what should be done at each stop."

Billy turned to Clay. "Your job, Clay, is to make sure that it'll all work and you all don't get killed doing it. Clay should have the final word in all operations. Clay, you're the boss in the field. Remember: Everybody comes home."

Rob Collings got up and paced around and then sat down. "No specific manpower, equipment, materiel in this outline? I figured you wouldn't get that far. I've got a list of my own, for you all to peruse."

"That's my boy. Always anticipating. Eric and Clay, you are in the presence of a tactical genius. Apologies for interrupting, Rob."

Collings continued. "First the team. Two munitions handlers: that's Eric and Clay. You'll work hand in glove with the HIT operator. He'll act in concert with the forward observer who will confirm the hits and make corrections. You'll need a DEWEMP operator and a driver-utility person. It's a trim and efficient six-man team."

Billy chimed in. "If you're gonna play, then play fast, and hard. Our WFJ Labs have the technology, weapons and equipment. It's the best, and through channels that I will not mention here, we have access to all of the latest military equipment that is available, and plenty of it, too.

WFJ Labs will modify everything for your use and add some new stuff. Full details on this when we meet again."

Collings suddenly got very serious. "That's all you need to know now. You'll travel light and deliver a lot of firepower. We'll get you down to our facilities for complete training with the equipment and run some drills."

Billy got up and walked around to where he could address Eric and Clay. Collings knew this was a sign that Billy was about to make a speech.

"Now, what you boys are proposin' could be classified as domestic terrorism. The real domestic terrorism masquerades in the guise of capitalism and free enterprise and that does much more damage to the environment, to the people, and to future generations. Our job, Rob's and mine, is to give you all the support we can. You guys are about to make a thought that I had a few years back a reality. And, I'm all for it. This country and the rest of the world are in very bad shape. The world needs to wake up soon, or all mankind will die off. I pray that you will be successful. Regardless whether you're successful, I have a plan in play that will change the world."

Billy turned and leaned with both hands on the table, facing all three men. "It'll be as easy as A-B-C. After you've completed these missions..."

Billy trailed off for a moment and looked at Rob. "I want you guys to be involved in my plan. But that's for later. Now, Rob has a strategy to get you out of here and down to our headquarters. No more talk now. We got a lot of thinking to do."

Billy stood tall. Rob got up as if on cue. "But rest assured, gentlemen, in the end, everything's gonna be all right. And that's a promise!"

Rob gave an almost imperceptible nod to Billy and pulled an envelope out of his briefcase.

Billy picked up his sunglasses and his tourist-style straw hat. "Gentlemen, this meeting's over."

Rob handed Clay an envelope and followed Billy out the door. The meeting was, in fact, over.

Amazed, Eric said. "They didn't even say goodbye."

"Billy's like that. When it comes down to business, he's all business. Nothing personal, Eric. Just the way he is."

Clay opened the envelope. The first words at the top of the page were:

DESTROY YOUR WRITTEN PLANS AND THIS MEMO AND ENVELOPE IMMEDIATELY AFTER READING.

Clay read the letter out loud to Eric.

Okay guys. You're in the big leagues now. Tomorrow at 08:00 be at the Mazatlan airport. Clean up and leave no trail. No need for passports; all taken care of. Our man will have a bright orange shirt and a white hat. He will take you to a small, unmarked jet. You will be blindfolded for the ride, so sit back and sleep. See you when you land.—R.C.

"Okay, Eric. We're in it now. How you doin'?"

"Scared shitless, you fool. We could get hurt or killed... But then, we just might pull it off, too. *Hoo-rah!*"

Fourteen

Semper Fi

William F. (Billy) Johnstone was a self-made billionaire. In Billy's first year at Great Southern Technical University, he met another student, Charles Gertz who almost drove him mad with his inventions and ideas. Charles was a genius, no doubt. Billy decided then and there to back the weird ideas of Charles Gertz.

Billy dropped out in his freshman year to join the Marines and fight in the Vietnam War. While he was in 'Nam, Billy sent half his monthly pay to Charles, and the rest to his mother. Robert (Rob) Collings, a tough and smart Marine, had been Billy's Captain in Vietnam.

When Billy came home from the war, he enrolled again at GSTU.

Charles was still there, working on his doctorate in biochemistry. Through those years, Billy continued to financially support Charles and his research projects.

Upon Billy's graduation, he and Charles formed WFJ Polybiotech Corporation. Through Billy's ideas, sales skills and fierce determination, coupled with the unique products developed by Dr. Gertz, the two became incredibly wealthy. It wasn't long before Billy hired Rob to be his right-hand man and the head of all security at WFJ Corporation.

Now, Billy and Rob had committed to use Billy's resources, their combined military training and Dr. Gertz's special inventive skills to aid Eric and Clay in this very interesting project.

The next morning, Eric and Clay got up at 5:00 a.m., showered, dressed and bolted down black coffee. Clay ditched their clothes in a dumpster away from the hotel. There was nothing in the clothing to identify them and he figured that some local would go dumpster diving and acquire a new wardrobe. Clay paid their hotel bill in cash, told the desk clerk they were going sight-seeing for the day and ordered a cab. If the hotel were to ask the cab driver he could honestly say that he took them to the airport. The hotel would think the *touristo gringos* changed their minds and moved on.

At the airport, as promised, a very polite latin man, Fernando, met them and ushered them to the waiting plane.

Eric and Clay buckled up and Fernando asked what they'd like to drink. Quickly he returned with big glasses of scotch and a little tray of appetizers. He warned them that within minutes of being airborne he would have to blindfold them. They understood.

As Eric and Clay relaxed on the plane, Agent G. David Edwards visited Eric's wife, Elaine.

Edwards did not accept the easy closure of this case. He was a dedicated, obsessive man. He steadfastly believed that both Eric and Clay could still be alive. In his off-duty hours, he conducted an unofficial investigation of his own.

David Edwards rang Elaine's doorbell. "Mrs. Atkins? CIA. Agent David Edwards. Yes, the Central Intelligence Agency, the CIA." He gave her his card and showed her his credentials.

Elaine invited him in.

"Now, Mrs. Atkins I don't want to alarm you, but I think that your husband may still be alive."

Elaine nearly fainted. "Uh...Could we sit down?" Elaine fell into a chair.

Edwards sat opposite Elaine. "I'm sorry to shock you, Mrs. Atkins. Are you all right?"

Elaine nodded, still stunned.

"I need to ask you a few questions. Have you had a phone call from your husband?"

Elaine responded quizzically, "No."

"Have you received any mail or messages from him?"

Elaine sat up straight, answering solidly. "No."

"Has anyone else called you or given you messages from or about him."

Elaine was emphatic and annoyed. "No."

"You've said no, but I ask you to be sure of your answers, Mrs. Atkins. This is very serious."

"Agent Edwards, my husband is dead. I am enduring the sorrow of my loss. I still have a great deal of difficulty...the anguish and grief. If you have evidence that my husband is still alive, please share it with me."

"Well, I don't have any hard evidence, but I have a policeman's hunch that the details of his death were too simple, too uncomplicated for me to believe. That's why I'm here and why I have continued this investigation."

Elaine was angry now. "You? Is this an official investigation?"

Edwards fumbled, looking down. "No, the FBI and CIA have closed the files on this matter." Then he sat up straight, confident. "But I have not. I intend to pursue it to my satisfaction." Edwards leaned in toward Elaine. "Now, I want real answers, Mrs. Atkins. The truth."

Elaine pulled back a bit. She wasn't sure what to make of this strangely intense man.

Edwards was more animated and spoke menacingly. "You are the beneficiary of a large insurance policy, one that could put you and your husband on easy street. I warn you that if you attempt to leave the country and take a large sum of money with you, you will be in violation of federal law. And, you should note that insurance fraud carries some very stiff jail time, Mrs. Atkins."

Elaine had had enough of his callous behavior and stood up. "Agent Edwards, I'm asking you to leave now. We have nothing more to say to each other. I will, however, call, email and write to your superiors about this unofficial interrogation and request that you be barred from annoying me further."

Edwards stood up and followed her to the door, then turned and said, "Mrs. Atkins that kind of threat has no effect. I'm a high-ranking officer. I do as I please. I'll be in touch with you again."

There must have been more in that whiskey than whiskey. As the plane descended for landing, Fernando gave Eric and Clay an injection. They awakened feeling quite refreshed. This was the beginning of Billy's magic tricks.

As they deplaned and looked around, they saw a high mountain range on one side and mountains about half that size on the other. Between the mountains was only a long, narrow landing strip in a natural valley.

Collings appeared. He greeted Eric, Clay and Fernando and motioned for the men to get into an open vehicle that had no steering wheel. It was electric and seemed to be guided by some unseen force. They headed at a brisk speed directly toward the face of the mountainside. Just as it seemed they would crash into it, an opening in the rocks appeared allowing them through.

Inside the mountain the car kept rolling down a long hall toward a metal clad wall, which also opened automatically, permitting the car into a room. The car stopped. The doors closed. The room descended. It was an elevator.

When the doors opened again, they were in a area with a thirty-foot ceiling that was longer than a football field. A man in a white lab coat walked toward them with a cheery greeting. It was Dr. Charles Gertz.

"Rob, Fernando, and this must be Eric and Clay. Glad to meet you both and welcome to my catacombs."

Rob handed Eric and Clay each a folder. "Not to interrupt you, Dr. Gertz, but I need to orient these guys. So, let's get down to work. In the folders, you'll find a list of what I think you'll need."

Eric and Clay took out the list and read through it as Rob explained:

Rob continued, "No personal arms. You don't want to engage, just destroy."

Eric shot a look at Clay.

Clay whispered, "It's cool."

Rob didn't take a breath. "First: sniper rifle. A trained sniper is a good idea because you might have to take out a few security people. In war someone has to die, you know, so he'll need the top of the line M31A1 rifle with a day/night scope and a silencer. His sole purpose will be as your forward observer.

"Second: The DEWEMP unit will knock out the computers, alarm systems, cell phones, CB and telephone systems. The power supply fits neatly in a backpack. This electronic gun is aimed with a scope just like a rifle. But, the DEWEMP can be fired wide angle or with the flip of switch it can pinpoint a target. Very advanced. It's an invention of Billy's and has been further developed in the WFJ labs by our Dr. Gertz. It's portable and very powerful.

"Third: No need to risk getting up close with C-4 and incendiary charges. You'll be using the latest military weapons that WFJ Labs have modified a bit. Dr. Gertz has done some modifications to increase the explosive power of this little missile. The Marines call it a 'Switchblade Drone.' We call it 'Hell-In-A-Tube;' HIT for short. It sets up like a mortar, has a built-in tripod and can be handled by one man. The HIT is very precise. As the drone launches, it opens its wings like a bird. The operator is able to see the target on a monitor fed from the side and forward cameras on the front of the drone. Using a joy-stick controlled guidance system, in real time, the operator can follow the drone from the launch on this monitor screen. Once the target is identified, the operator flies the little missile to its final destination and causes it to detonate. Total weight of the HIT drone and firing tube is about five and a half pounds. Dozens of them will be packed in your equipment container."

Clay asked, "What kind of accuracy does this thing have?"

"From a range of two miles, the HIT will give you accuracy all day long and blow up whatever you target. It's a kick-ass weapon. Delivers incendiary, anti-personnel or high explosives, and some special charges, too. It's speedy, accurate and almost impossible to detect."

Rob waited to see whether there were more questions.

Eric nodded for him to continue.

"Fourth: night vision. All of your operations should be done at night. Fewer people to be injured and less chance of being observed. So, night vision for all is mandatory. You'll be using the AN/PVS-14 device. It's the best and it is very adjustable to almost all light conditions.

"Fifth: communication. Again, WFJ labs has a two-way radio system that doesn't use normal available airwaves. Even the military can't find the wave-length on our units. Your forward observer will be using this new radio.

"Sixth: clothing. Black coveralls, hoods and gloves over civilian clothes applicable to the weather conditions."

Clay remarked snidely, "That's all?"

Rob ignored him. "Summary: All of this equipment will be delivered to a rendezvous point for each operation. Using a special GPS app on your mobile phone you'll be able to find it. The Hell Tubes, control unit, sniper rifle, radio, DEWEMP and clothing will all be contained in one low profile case for each operation. After you've completed your mission, just put it all back in the container and use the 'Gertz Juice' to destroy your equipment, and then exit quickly."

Eric asked, "Gertz juice?"

"The 'Gertz Juice' is another invention, designed to reduce anything to a mass of goo. It will make the fed boys and their forensics people go crazy."

"Uh-huh." Clay was beginning to put things together.

Rob continued. "In each selected location, all materials will be provided to you so you'll have everything necessary to handle that job. In each shipment, you'll have new sets of maps and plans, as well as new ID for the next mission. There will be no trail of airline tickets, hotels or car rentals. You'll be a brand new group of guys each time."

Eric was enthusiastic. "That's incredible, Rob. Perfect solutions. We won't have to carry anything, just go to the rendezvous point, get new equipment and plans, and blow up the target. Great. Great. Fantastic thinking, guys."

Clay looked around the room. "So, you got some sort of demo set up for us?"

Dr. Gertz spoke. "I'm going to show you a couple of little pieces that we have engineered. We're selling these to the U. S. military at this time. First, we have the new M31A1 sniper rifle, which is a top of line weapon. It uses a .338 Lapua Magnum cartridge and with a day or night scope it is quite accurate at two miles.

"And this is our innovative Directed Energy Weapon Electro-Magnetic Pulse gun. We call it the DEWEMP. It will immediately knock out all electrical and electronic equipment at up to a one-and-a-half-mile range. The light-weight capacitor back pack will allow for over fifty blasts of energy. We have designed this system to allow the long distance destruction of radios, computers, car engines, etc. Using the scope sighting and night vision this unit will be invaluable to your project.

"The radio that your sniper and forward spotter will use is on a wavelength that even the military doesn't know about and transmits the coordinates in encrypted digital code.

"And, in addition, we are in the process of developing many more useful tools for you to use."

Dr. Gertz moved toward a long table. Many items were displayed with little descriptive cards on each one.

"We've designed a number of very special explosive charges for the HIT drones. Each one is intended to do a specific job. All have spike tips that will penetrate up to a half inch of steel or they can be used to make a contact explosion, or an aerial burst, as you may need.

"After you have disabled the security systems, radios and telephones with the DEWEMP you will launch this WHITE missile. It will explode in the air and drop by parachute emitting a siren noise and deliver warnings and evacuation orders in English, Spanish, German and French. It will continue to repeat the messages for three more minutes after it lands and then it will self-destruct.

"This YELLOW drone is very interesting. It has a needle-like tip and flying it up to one thousand feet and using gravity it will be able to penetrate the top of an oil or gasoline storage tank. Once inside, compressed gas explodes the multiple rounds which contain a chemical that will neutralize the gasoline or oil. The petrol is thereby made unusable and not able to be sold.

"This needle-tipped BLUE round will be used for the chemical and pharmaceutical tanks and will neutralize the contents very quickly, as well.

"I've been in contact with your 'Fiendish Freddy,' Eric. He's given me the formulas for these neutralizers. He's right on the money. We produced them in our labs. They work!

"And this GREEN round will normally be used as an aerial burst although it can penetrate, too. It can be set for delayed explosion inside food factories or slaughter houses. It contains a deadly poison, similar to Sarin gas, which will kill all livestock, pigs, beef, chickens—humans, too—within one to three minutes. The gas dissipates very quickly and becomes totally harmless within ten minutes. What's more, it will contaminate the animal flesh and cause it to become inedible by humans or animals. It's quite effective.

"Again, thank you, Freddy. You know, Eric, I'd sure like to get Fred Masinga to come out here and work with me. He has an excellent mind and one we could really use. I'm going to ask Billy to bring him on board. Yes, yes, I will…

"Well, moving on now, this RED sharp-tipped round is designed to penetrate roof tops and explode inside using a delayed fuse. It can also be set for aerial or impact burst. This baby is a true WFJ invention. By combining our secret explosive with Thermite, it becomes a super incendiary, as well as, a very potent and volatile bomb. It is without a doubt the most powerful explosive known today. This will really impress you with the damage it does.

"We have color-coded each drone. The WHITE one to deliver the evacuation warnings. YELLOW for the gasoline neutralizer. BLUE are the chemical and pharmaceutical neutralizers. GREEN is for the livestock and RED is the high explosive and incendiary round. All neatly packaged in six pound bombs to do the jobs you may require them to do."

Rob Collings added. "Impressive work, Dr. Gertz. Well, I think we're done for today, people."

Eric and Clay were dismissed, returning to their sleeping quarters to shower and shave for dinner.

Fifteen

Seeing Elaine Again

Eric and Clay lay awake in their sleeping quarters. It had been an intense day. The fact that they were really going to do this was still sinking in. It was a quiet night. The moonlight was bright, casting shadows in the room.

Eric asked Clay, "Remember that scene with George Scott standing in the water? It looked like the dolphin was saying something to him."

"Yeah," responded blankly. "What's your point?"

"After I met Dr. John Lilly I asked him if he knew, or could guess, what the dolphin said—even though it was just a movie. He thought for a while and gave me his answer. I wrote it down. I've kept it in my wallet all these years. It's the reason I'm doing this."

Clay was intrigued. "So, did Lilly really have conversations with dolphins? I mean, did they really understand him? Do they think like us?"

Eric got up on one elbow and faced Clay. "Well, he said they did. First, he taught them some English words and they, in turn, taught him how to speak dolphin. Sort of."

Eric sat up. "It took him years to just get to simple conversations, no real grammar, but they could understand each other. Most importantly, he said they could communicate ideas. John Lilly was convinced that given time, he could hold in-depth conversations with all cetacea using the dolphins as interpreters, and maybe he could discover valid facts about man's origins and his relationship with the oceans. Unfortunately, the US Navy got in his way. He got pretty disgusted and disillusioned and he quit trying. Sad."

"Man. And now, we're destroying the environment for them and us..." Clay turned toward Eric. "So, Eric. Tell me what the dolphin said."

Eric got his wallet and removed the plastic laminated piece of paper. "Okay, I got it. Here is what Dr. Lilly told me the dolphin might have said: Water life. Man hurt water. Water dead. Man dead."

After a few days of intense instruction, Eric requested that he be allowed to return to San Diego to see Elaine. He pleaded with Billy, telling him that once the operation was started he knew he wouldn't be able to see her for a long time. He wanted her to know that he was alive.

Collings warned "You going to the West Coast puts not just you in great jeopardy, but this project. You can't just call her, or send her a letter or even email her. You know the FBI and CIA are monitoring not just Elaine, but all of your friends."

Eric wasn't giving up. "But, what about Freddy? Fred Masinga. He's ex-marine."

Billy acquiesced. "You must follow my exact instructions."

Rob shot Billy a look.

Billy responded. "I'm going to be quite exact about the terms of this trip, or we're out. You'll be disguised from the time you leave until you return. You'll travel by WFJ private jet to an airfield outside of San Diego, and then to the selected meeting place by car. Rob, get a message to Freddy and work out the details. This meeting's over."

Billy walked out.

Eric was elated.

Rob Collings was not pleased.

Eric flew to the little airport and a car was waiting for him. Billy's man gave Eric the directions and keys to a vehicle. Eric drove from the airport to the meeting place.

Freddy was waiting for Eric on a bench near the Central Library on the UC San Diego campus. As Eric approached him, Freddy got up and began walking along side Eric.

"Glad you signaled, ol' man. With that disguise, I'd never have recognized you. Glad to see you're alive and well. Dammit, Eric what have you done?"

Eric, stumbling on his words, nearly gushed forth the details of the boat wreck, the killings, the Mexican adventure, Billy's help and everything he could think of.

This meeting with his friend Freddy reinforced that Eric was still a part of a world that he wanted very much. But, he knew he had to let go.

"Elaine, Freddy! How is she? Where will I meet her?"

"I've been given specific instructions for your meeting place. But, what do you plan to do, Eric?"

"I'm going to stop the major polluters. The EPA won't, but we will. Freddy, I need you. Come on board with us."

"My heart's not good, Eric, or I'd join you. I'll do what I can to help. I've been in contact with Dr. Gertz." Freddy handed Eric an envelope. "I have some recipes here for him. Don't worry about taking them with you. They won't mean anything to anybody but Gertz."

The two sat and talked for quite some time, old friends hurrying to share everything important with each other.

Abruptly, Freddy stopped the conversation and told Eric it was time to meet with Elaine. He gave him the exact location. It was on the beach near Scripps Pier. They hugged. Freddy wished him well, and walked away.

Eric watched his dearest friend disappear into the eucalyptus trees, not knowing whether he would see Freddy again.

Quickly Eric went up the path to the parking area and headed the car toward the beach.

He drove down toward the Pacific Ocean. Past Scripps Pier, there on the rocks, he saw Elaine.

She watched the car park and intuitively walked briskly toward it and got in.

"Oh, Eric." She through her arms around his neck. They shared a long, warm embrace. Elaine pulled back and gazed quizzically at Eric. "Quite the disguise: the beard and hair color change?"

Eric drank in her glowing face. He didn't want this moment to end.

Elaine reached over and squeezed his hand knowingly. "I've missed you..." She decided not to tell Eric about her encounter with Edwards.

Eric squeezed Elaine's hand. They sat for a moment looking into one another's eyes, holding hands.

Then, Eric started the car and drove them to *Walken's by the Sea*, a place that had given them many good evenings. Even though he was disguised, Eric was careful not to be seated at their usual table.

The waiter, Karl, who had served them many times, was again going to serve them tonight.

The waiter leaned in to speak to Elaine. "Mrs. Atkins. So sorry to hear of your loss. Eric and you were two of my favorite people. I'll miss him very much." Standing straighter, he addressed them both. "I hope that you will enjoy your evening."

Eric was surprised at how good the disguise was. It fooled the waiter completely.

Elaine said. "Karl, we're going to the La Jolla Playhouse tonight, so I think we'll only have time for a glass of wine and an appetizer."

They ordered and relaxed.

Eric sat across from her and made sure not to hold Elaine's hands. Even though he was dying to kiss her, he restrained himself.

They finished the dinner quickly and left saying good night to Karl, the waiter, who still did not recognize Eric.

Eric drove down to La Jolla Shores. They got out of the car and rested on a grassy spot near the beach.

"You know, I went nuts after I heard you were dead. Now that you're here...You have to tell me what the hell is going on. Why did you pretend to be dead?"

Eric wanted to tell her everything but knew that if interrogated, she could be made to talk. He carefully fabricated his answer. "Well, beautiful, if I'm dead you become a very rich girl. Then, when the time is right, you and I will go to South America and live like royalty. I took advantage of that boat accident to play dead and get away from all of it. It's just that simple, and it will work."

"What?" She knew something wasn't right, that Eric wasn't telling her everything. "And how long before we see each other again?"

"A few months. Or maybe sooner…"

"Are you sure about this, babe?"

Eric pulled her closer. Enveloping her in his arms, he kissed her tenderly, lovingly, passionately.

The moon over the ocean and the warm night allowed them to make love in a most sincere way. Elaine didn't like the idea of a long separation. But she trusted him. There was a good reason for all of this. She was sure of it. Now for her part, she was going to give him something to remember, and hopefully hasten his return.

About 2:00 a.m., Eric told Elaine that he had to leave. He assured her that he would make arrangements for her to hear from him through Freddy and that they would be together again very soon.

Unbeknownst to either of them, Karl, the waiter at *Walken's By the Sea*, had been visited the day before by CIA Agent G. David Edwards. Edwards requested Karl's help and showed him pictures of Clay, Freddy, Eric and Elaine. Edwards gave Karl a phony oath and told him he was now a deputized CIA agent. Agent Edwards left the pictures and told Karl to call him if he ever saw any of them.

The next evening, as ordered, Karl called Agent Edwards. "Agent K reporting, sir. Mrs. Atkins was in the restaurant with a man tonight. No, it was not Eric, or any of the other men in the pictures. I've never seen this man before. I listened for Elaine to call him by name, but she didn't. They only had appetizers and wine. She said they were going to the La Jolla Playhouse to see a show."

"Good work Agent K. Continue to keep your eyes open."

A few days after Elaine and Eric had met, CIA agent Edwards went back to the Atkins house.

Elaine was not happy to see him. Reluctantly she allowed him to come into her home.

"Good afternoon, Mrs. Atkins. I told you I'd be back."

"Yes. You're kind of like a hungry dog in that way…"

Edwards ignored the slight and followed her into the living room, sitting across from her.

"I received a call from one of our operatives. He tells me you and Eric had dinner at *Walken's By the Sea* the other night. He observed you closely."

"Your 'operative' is mistaken."

"Why don't you just tell me the truth, Mrs. Atkins. Where is Eric?"

With some irritation, she answered. "That man was not Eric, Agent Edwards. He is a friend and we went to the theater that night. I think your man is making all this up."

"Okay, tell me who this man is. Give me his name and we can quickly discredit what 'my man' has told me."

"I will not tell you his name. I don't want him dragged into your stupid games. Again, I ask you to leave and stop bothering me. I'll say nothing more."

"I'll leave, but not just yet. I've also met with Professor Fred Masinga. You know, he told me everything. How Eric told him of his plans to stage his death and how you and Eric would cash in the insurance money and leave the country. Masinga will testify to all of that in court. Together with the testimony from our operative, you're done, Elaine. Now tell me where Eric is and we'll close this case."

"That's ridiculous, I've known Freddy for years. I can't believe that he would say such things. You're lying. You're lying. Eric is dead. He's dead!"

Elaine was very angry. She stood up and waved her arms at him, shooing him toward the door, screaming loudly, "Get the hell out of here, you fucking bastard. And don't ever come back! Get out!"

Edwards, infuriated, instinctively hit her squarely on the jaw. Elaine fell immediately, striking her head on the corner of the fireplace hearth.

Edwards bent down to Elaine's motionless body and checked her pulse. Blood from the wound on the back of her head oozed out onto the floor. Her eyes were open, frozen in terror. "Oh god oh god oh god. She's dead!"

When Eric returned to the WFJ complex, Clay and Rob Collings had already selected and acquired the specialized team members. They were all experienced people.

The next morning Rob assembled Eric, Clay and the new team and brought them all to the big room. As Rob called out the team members' names, each stepped forward to salute and shake hands with Eric and Clay.

Each team member was to be addressed by his or her first name. Clay and Eric were to be known only as Number One and and Number Two, respectively. Only Billy, Rob and Gertz would know their real names.

Rob explained the duty of each team member. Number One (Clay) and Number Two (Eric) would act as the munitions handlers. Jake (Kaminsky) would be the artillery man and in control of HIT drones. Ian (McAllister) would act as forward spotter and sniper. George (Hubel) would man the DEWEMP gun. Saya (Goldmyer) would be the driver-utility person.

This, then, was their small, yet effective, assault team. After Eric met with his people, he gave Dr. Gertz the envelope containing the detailed formulas from Freddy.

Dr. Gertz looked over the papers and exclaimed: "'Fiendish Freddy' is as good as his reputation. In these few pages, he's quickly solved several of the problems that were on my plate. He's correct in every detail.

I can manufacture the stuff right here, and in very short order, too. I've got to get Freddy out here to help us."

Charles Gertz had become the "Q" of the operation, relishing every moment of his involvement. It took him away from the mundane development of WFJ bio-projects. He was having a great time playing with these modern "007s."

Rob Collings spoke up. "Now, Number One and Number Two, we want to show you how the HIT works. Everyone, all of you, let's go outside for the demo."

They walked down a long tunnel, opened a blast door and then took an elevator up that opened to another tunnel. As the last big door opened, they were outside.

The test area was about the size of two football fields. At the far end, against a solid rock wall were several barrels used as targets. Scorch marks on the wall gave evidence that this site was used to test explosives.

Rob informed them. "Jake was trained to use drones by the Marines. After he mustered out, he came to work in our munitions unit. He's been out here every day practicing with our version of the Switchblade, the HIT, the Hell-in-a-Tube drone. He's very good and seldom misses."

Rob directed their attention toward the rock wall. "Way down there are many big plastic barrels of water. Jake will attempt to take each of them out. Watch closely."

This was the first time Eric, Clay and the others had ever seen the HIT drone in action.

Jake removed the computer control unit and a RED missile from a large storage container. He opened the tripod and made the HIT drone ready and launched it to the air. Using the monitor screen and joy-sticks he guided the little missile high in the sky and then deftly brought it down to hit one of the barrels.

A loud explosion and then water erupted everywhere.

Clay stated. "A direct hit, with the HIT. Good on, Jake!

Rob laughed at the joke. "We are using very light charges in these drones and water in the barrels. Much heavier explosives will be used in the actual scenarios and you can imagine when it contacts flammable materials. Big noise. Lots of fire. *Hoo-rah.*"

After a few more launches of the HIT, Rob asked Dr. Gertz to demonstrate his "Juice."

The test was on a couple of rifles and some metal boxes. Amazingly, it all melted away and left a hole in the concrete.

Gertz smiled. "Well, it does work, as you can see. I've only used a little or the destruction could continue on through the earth to its center and right down into China!"

They all chuckled at his humor.

"Well not really. But we've developed exacting instructions for its use. You must use it as directed…"

Rob Colling's mobile phone rang. He turned away from the group to answer it. He said nothing into the phone, held it to his ear briefly, then quickly flipped it closed.

Rob turned back toward the group and interrupted the teaching session. Brusquely, he told Eric and Clay to follow him and turned over the rest of the team to Dr. Gertz.

Rob, Eric and Clay traveled through a maze of tunnels and to another level of the huge complex to a hidden room. Billy wanted to begin the planning stage of the operations and had set aside the entire afternoon and evening for that purpose.

Billy was waiting for them at a long table. "Eric, Clay please tell me again everything about this project."

Eric and Clay looked at one another. Eric said, "You know everything. We haven't held anything back."

Billy continued. "Sorry to make you repeat it but I need to know what you know. We must be on the same page."

Eric restated his mission quite passionately. "We must stop the perpetrators of this pollution and inform the public of how they are being poisoned just to make more profits for the big corporations. I do not want these missions to further pollute or damage the environment. I only want to punish the corporations and hurt their cash flow, maybe even put them out of business. Hopefully these raids will teach other smaller violators and potential violators that they are not above reproach. I want to 'inspire' them to mend their ways..."

Billy stopped him. "...Yes, yes. I certainly acknowledge that your reasons for engaging in this project are very altruistic. Quite appropriate, Eric. But now I am asking for a specific plan of operation."

"My idea is to simply destroy the operations of the most flagrant EPA, FDA, USDA violators. The plans for whom to hit, when and where and the damage I think we need to inflict are detailed here." Eric took some papers out his jacket and tossed them onto the table in front of Billy.

As Billy, Collings and Clay read the plans, Eric mentally recalled how when he was in his twenties he turned away from aggressive activism and advocated non-violent solutions to the great problems of pollution. He hated hostility and war and killing. It was truly strange to him that now he was involved in re-learning how to destroy and blow-up things. "What incredible irony," he thought.

Billy stood up. "Planning. Execution. Escape. This is what I want. Some fine work, Eric and Clay. You boys have got the targets and strategy, now let's plan the tactics to do this thing."

Since the targets for the missions had already been determined, while the assault team was being trained Billy's people were busy delivering the equipment containers to rented venues throughout the country. The selected buildings, large or small, were within close proximity to the targets in isolated areas, free of surveillance cameras or gates.

At each building, new locks were put on the doors and the windows were blacked out with plastic. A power pack for battery lighting was included in each equipment container.

During this planning session with Billy and Rob it was decided that prior to each operation, a "warning" message would be issued to hopefully prevent unnecessary deaths during the raids. Billy's people were in charge of the messaging. Using a PR-style computer program, mass press releases were broadcast and sent over the internet to all media, big and small.

In addition, the same email messages were sent to the CIA, FBI, NSA, DOD and POTUS, as well as the headquarters of every major corporation who might have violated the EPA, FDA, USDA regulations. These corporations were the major violators and the primary targets.

Since the location of the planned destruction was not mentioned, the media would put the entire nation on alert.

The warning messages would be sent out at 9:00 p.m., EST, giving little time for military defense of an unknown target.

It was determined that after the first mission, the team would follow up each week with other targets in different geographic locations.

These raids would cause unrest and further uncertainty for the government, as they would not know the size or scope of the "terrorist" organization.

Full national media attention was assured. They could gleefully imagine the chaos and confusion that would ensue at the corporate and government levels.

Eric felt that his plan was going to work. He was happy and excited that all was moving forward.

Now, it was reality time. Billy and his vast resources would support Eric and Clay with the munitions and equipment that they needed.

However, Billy had plans of his own.

Sixteen

The Mission Begins

Billy called a special meeting with Collings and Bob Sully, his IT man and head of the computer division.

"Here's what I want you to do, Bob. Destroy the computer infrastructure of AP&G at their home office in San Francisco and in their New York office, as well. Can you do it without being discovered?"

Bob Sully did not hesitate in his answer. "Of course, Billy. We can hack into their mainframe and send specifically designed Trojan malware, a bot, worm or a destructive virus that will knock everything out. However, since we don't know their backup capability, we should be prepared to do it over and over. Keep in mind, though, repeated assaults could possibly lead to exposure."

Billy stood up. "Bob, will one hit do them in?"

"It sure will cause damage. Total destruction? Possibly."

"Understand, in the highly volatile world of gas and oil production, one surprise hit would be enough to cripple them financially and probably put them out of business." Billy thought for a moment. "No, repeated attacks are prohibitive. We don't want to risk being found out. One hit should be the frosting on the cake. I want you to get on this immediately, Bob. You have one week. This meeting's over."

Back on the West Coast, Freddy was visited by Agent Edwards. With some unsuccessful amateur 'Columbo' tactics, Edwards tried to trap Freddy.

"So, let me get this straight. You know Eric Atkins, but you haven't see him lately. Is that right Mr. Masinga?"

"You can't be that stupid. Do you think I believe in ghosts? He's dead. Of course, I haven't seen him!"

"Well, we think he's alive and only pretending to be dead, So, my question is appropriate, Mr. Masinga. I could arrest you and take you in for interrogation, you know. Furthermore, Mr. Masinga, I've spoken with Elaine Atkins. She's implicated you in this alleged insurance fraud…"

"Fuck you. That's a lie. If you, Agent Edwards, and the CIA, represent my tax dollars at work, I want a refund. Get the hell out of here. And don't come back until you have a warrant."

A few days later Freddy learned of Elaine's death. He called Dr. Gertz's private number. Eric was summoned and allowed to talk with Freddy. They would only have a few minutes to talk.

"Eric, I'm sorry to tell you…Uh. Listen. I'm just going to say it. Hell, Elaine is dead. It appears to be an accident. She was found by the EMP unit who were anonymously called by someone."

"What? That can't be right… Not Elaine. It's got to be a mistake."

"I know. I know, man. It's… She fell and hit her head on the fireplace. The hospital called me to identify the body."

Eric was shaking. "This isn't happening. You're wrong. You're wrong, man !" He shouted into the phone, "Not Elaine! Elaine…"

Freddy tried to talk him down. "Eric! Eric, listen to me! I don't think it's as simple as it appears. Pay attention, man! Look, there might be foul play involved."

He only heard half of what Freddy was saying. "Elaine? My dear, sweet Elaine, dead?"

"Eric. Eric! Listen, we don't have much time to talk. A CIA Agent, a David Edwards, came to my house, grilled me, tried to pressure me. I told him to fuck off and leave. Eric, they think you're alive. He said that he had visited Elaine a few days before he came to see me and wasn't satisfied with her answers, or my answers, either. Maybe he went back to see Elaine. Maybe there was a scuffle. Maybe he hit her..."

Eric was furious. "He what?"

"Who knows? These government guys can pull anything. It might have been murder, Eric..."

The phone abruptly went dead.

Dazed, Eric stood with the phone in his hand. He was a shattered man. His reason for living, his wife, was dead.

Even though he was emotionally devastated, Eric was more determined than ever to complete these eco-terrorist missions. He no longer had anything to lose. Nothing to live for. No one to come home to.

With a vengeance, he now had a new goal: To kill, G. David Edwards.

GENERAL RELEASE

WARNING: Sometime soon we will attack and destroy the offices and all operations at one of the well-known companies who have been continually cited by the EPA, FDA, OSHA as major and habitual environmental polluters.

You know who you are. You know what you have been doing is wrong and deadly. Now, you will be stopped.

WE ARE AMERICANS! (not foreign terrorists) We are citizens who are fed-up with your poisoning of our air, water, food and environment. We will tolerate no more.

We are angry. We are many.

We intend to put you out of business.

NOTICE: You do not have time to locate the High Explosives planted at your operations, nor do you know where or when we will strike.

No humans should be hurt from the planned destruction of your facilities, if you alert them now.

Moments prior to our attack we will again alert your personnel to evacuate. We do not seek human fatalities.

However, anyone deciding to remain on your property will be assuming the risk of injury or even death.

YOU HAVE BEEN WARNED!

This media release was designed to attract attention to their purpose, but not to reveal the actual target.

The first raid objective was to be the gigantic AP&G oil and chemical refinery near Houston, Texas.

The team flew into Houston and took separate shuttles to different hotels. For security, only Number One and Number Two knew where each of the hotels were located.

Early in the morning, Eric called Saya's mobile phone and gave her a location where he and Clay would wait for her to retrieve them.

Saya drove the van she had rented at the airport and, as ordered, Saya arrived on time. Eric placed a hood on Saya's head and told her to lie down in the back of the van on the floor. Eric and Clay got into the car. Clay got behind the wheel and drove to the hotels to pick up the other three.

Although Saya had been a member of the elite Israeli Maglan Commando unit and had the highest clearance and trust, she would never know where Eric, Clay and the others were staying. This was a security measure ensuring that only Eric and Clay new the whereabouts of their team.

As each one of the men entered the van, Eric gave them hoods and told them to lie down on the floor in the back of the van.

It was a little past nine o'clock in the evening. They headed to a warehouse just south of Humble, Texas.

This warehouse had been rented by Billy's people and the promised big container crate of weapons and equipment was set on the floor of the little warehouse.

They assembled around and Eric was the first to speak. "Our target is AP&G Oil and its largest refinery in the United States. AP&G has been a consistent EPA and OSHA violator. This huge refining operation has a shameful history of explosions, spills, as well as, the deaths and maiming of many of its employees. It merely pays the EPA and OSHA fines levied against it, and does nothing to correct its methods of operation. It is a major polluter. The AP&G mega oil refinery is capable of processing over 500,000 barrels of crude oil per day and is located on more than 2,000 acres, surrounded by one of the biggest gasoline and petrochemical "tank farms" ever assembled. Oil, and the refining of oil itself, is a huge polluter and in producing gasoline and diesel fuel for internal combustion engines, this process and the resulting fuel product become a major contributor of CO^2 emissions. In addition, the runoff has severely polluted the Gulf of Mexico and the ground water and air for miles around. This one needs to be hurt, and hurt bad! In doing so we will land a severe financial blow to big oil."

Clay handed Saya, the driver, the approach and exit routes, and to Jake, the detailed target plans. On the top of the supply crate Clay spread out a big map of the area showing the routes and targets for all to see.

Clay instructed them. "Each one of you please take the time to go over these plans and look at the map. I want your questions now, not later. No fuck ups. Next, we'll load the van. Then there'll be a quiz to see if you know what the hell you're doing."

Thanks to the WFJ aerial pictures and maps, Eric and Clay were able to do some very accurate target research. The maps allowed them to grid and pin-point their targets in a military fashion. With the accompanying digital photos, it allowed them to understand the terrain and confirm the assault plans and refine the escape routes.

They all studied the map and photos and entered into a productive and quiet discussion of the mission. This refinery was just a huge disaster waiting to happen. They were all mindful of the potential conflagration that could occur if they bungled their plan in any way.

It was a cloudless night. Visibility was very clear.

About three-quarters of a mile from the refinery, Saya dropped Jake, Eric, Clay and the munitions container at the designated fire-base. Without delay, Jake set up his radio, turned on his computer and got ready.

Saya drove to the forward position site. It was less than a quarter of a mile away from the refinery. She dropped off Ian, and George. These two would be stationed on a little rise so both men had a good view of the refinery.

George pulled up his scope to scan the area. He related his observations to Ian, who was using his scope, too. Ian confirmed the situation as "quiet" and called an "all-clear" back to the fire center.

Then George started popping off DEWEMP flashes at the objective so that silently and effectively all communications at the refinery were systematically rendered inoperable.

Eric and Clay prepared the YELLOW shells to be launched. They hurried, as they needed to begin firing the missiles to remain on schedule.

The first targets were the gasoline storage tanks nearest the crackling columns. These tanks needed to be made non-flammable first so as not to cause a major fire.

Information for the first storage tank was called in from Ian. Jake read the calculations and dialed the coordinates into the computer for the first salvo. When he was ready, he launched one missile, then another. Using the joy-stick controls, Jake guided the HIT drones' silent glide through the night sky high into the air, then retracted their wings transforming them into missiles. Suddenly, they dropped in dive-bomber fashion toward the storage tanks, easily piercing the tops.

Jake quickly reported to Eric and Clay that his little "needles" had squarely hit their targets.

Ian gave Jake new clearance for the next tank. One, then two drones were launched. Again, the hits were positively confirmed. Time after time they launched and silently penetrated the storage tanks making the petrol unusable.

Clay exclaimed. "Rob wasn't kidding us. The Hell In Tubes operated exactly as advertised. Keep going, Jake."

Eric and Clay began sweating inside the black coveralls and mask. Prepping the Hell In Tubes for Jake to launch was exhausting work. They had spent over ten minutes firing the YELLOW drones into the gasoline tanks.

Then they ceased. As planned, thirty tanks had been penetrated and the gasoline and oil contained in those huge storage containers had been rendered useless.

They did not target every tank. Clay had designed a pattern. He thought that not knowing which tanks held good product and which ones did not would add to the confusion.

But, the job was not done. Next were the petrochemical storage tanks. They repeated their tactics using the BLUE drones, which, again, successfully spoiled the contents of each tank.

After hitting ten tanks, they stopped firing.

All this destruction had gone on without anyone knowing what was happening. It was silent and very efficient.

George continued the DEWEMP barrage stopping forklifts and trucks in their tracks as they moved about the refinery.

Now, Ian's message to the fire center was "all clear."

Clay ordered Jake to launch the WHITE warning drones.

Because the area was so large, four WHITE missiles were used. As the drones exploded in the air they could hear the sirens and warning messages.

Bombs have been placed everywhere in this refinery. They will explode in one minute. Evacuate the refinery now. Get far away from the refinery. Leave now. Run for your lives. Bombs have been placed everywhere in this refinery. They will explode in one minute. Evacuate the refinery, now. Get far away from the refinery. Leave now. Run for your lives!

The message repeated and repeated. Clay waited.

Ian's radio text transmission reported that the workers were scattering in every direction on foot.

After waiting 3 minutes. Ian's all clear came through.

Now they were ready for the final destruction. "Get the RED ones ready." Clay ordered.

Jake set the coordinates for the big cracking columns and pipe systems at the heart of the refinery. He launched two RED drones high in the sky. The tiny bomb-missiles were skillfully guided to the target and upon landing they detonated.

Loud explosions and tremendous fire erupted.

Clay cried out, "Direct hit, Jake. Keep 'em coming."

Another and another of the RED drones were rapidly fired at different sets of cracking columns. The vast network of pipes became a twisted and burning mass of steel.

"Now, get one of the big tanks near the blaze, Jake."

Again, the accuracy and artillery synchronization was perfect. The RED drone was launched and the torrent of destruction continued. The area was flooded with burning gasoline causing more explosions.

Clay shouted. "On target. Last one, gunner."

Jake set the coordinates for the fifth RED drone and launched it toward another huge storage tank near the burning mass of pipes.

It was time to depart. Clay barked. "Where is Saya? We need to get the hell out of here!"

Saya had picked up Ian and George and was quickly heading back to the fire center for Jake, Eric and Clay.

The night sky was brilliantly lit up with flashes and flares, followed by many hot blazing balls of fire that rose hundreds of feet in the air. It could be seen for miles. The refinery was enveloped in gasoline and oil fire and it appeared as though it was the end of the world.

The total elapsed time from the beginning of the drone launches to the last was less than 15 minutes. No deaths, just serious destruction of one of the world's largest petrol refineries.

Soon, distant sirens could be heard as fire, police and ambulances raced toward the refinery.

Saya arrived at the firebase with Ian and George.

All of the maps, plans, old IDs, plane tickets, full and empty HITs, the sniper rifle, night spotting glasses, the DEWEMP, radios and computers were thrown back into the container crate. The items were then treated with the "Gertz Juice" and immediately dissolved.

Clay clicked the lever on each 'juice can' and threw them into what was left of the container crate. The cans self-destructed and became part of the hot gooey mass.

The team leaped into the van and Saya headed out of the area toward the designated drop-off points in Houston.

The raid had gone just as planned. They were elated. Eric now knew this could be done, anywhere, anytime.

Clay gave the new IDs and plane tickets to all of them and one by one they were dropped at bus stops. Each was now on their own to get back to their respective hotels.

After dropping them off, Saya delivered the van to the closed car rental lot and took an airport shuttle to her hotel.

Other than Clay and Eric, none of them knew where any of the others were staying that night.

Once the team was back at their respective hotels they took off their clothes and shoes and stuffed them into the hotel plastic dry cleaning bags and put them in the hallway trash bins.

They had been instructed to take showers and carefully scrub every part of their bodies to remove any lingering traces of explosives. Then they dressed in fresh clothes. They did not want to set off the explosive detectors or rile-up the dogs or men at the airport when they departed.

All through the night the media reported about the fire at the refinery. The media only covered the fire and had no opinion about its origin.

The next morning, Eric and Clay were having coffee and danish and leisurely watching the television. When they heard the sketchy comments and wild pronouncements on the morning news, they smiled and understood how well they had done their job.

Not a word from the targeted AP&G Oil Company. Not a word from the government. Nothing about whether there might be other targets. No words meant they were all taken by surprise and were now forced to wait and see whether another attack on another refinery would happen.

That same morning in his office at the Complex, Billy was reading an internet news site. He spoke with modest elation to Rob Collings. "Yeah, yeah, Rob, they blew it all up. Good mission and as the *coup de grace* we destroyed the computer infrastructure of AP&G Oil in San Francisco and New York. Bob did a helluva job. AP&G Oil is severely injured, might even be finished! Now, on to the next one, and further success!"

For each new target, Billy's people had provided the team with new names, occupations, credit cards and photo identification, all of which could not be traced.

Billy had cleverly set up his own travel agency and therefore was able to initiate booking of all the air flights, car rentals and hotels from a secret location.

The next day, another media release was issued.

GENERAL RELEASE:

SUMMARY: Last night we destroyed the crude oil, gasoline, diesel fuel and petrochemicals in the storage tanks of AP&G Oil refinery in South Texas. AP&G Oil is a major and habitual ecological violator and has been cited time after time by OSHA and the EPA.

AP&G Oil has done nothing to correct the pollution caused by their refining processes, or to fix the leaking of petroleum and petrochemicals into the Gulf of Mexico and the local aquifers.

Therefore, since AP&G Oil has not complied with the EPA, we as citizens, have severely penalized them.

AP&G Oil Is Out Of Business!

WARNING: If gasoline prices go up because of this attack more refineries will suffer the same fate. If the U.S. government will not stop the rampant pollution by the big oil corporations, we will!

Expect more!

Three days after the refinery mission, each of Eric's team drove to the Houston airport, dropped off their rented cars and separately departed on different airlines, at different times. Two of them left early in the afternoon, two late afternoon, Eric and Clay in the evening.

Their next stop was Denver, Colorado.

With exceptional planning, they each arrived in Denver, with rental cars waiting, and hotels secured.

Seventeen

Cat and Mouse

Meanwhile, in Los Angeles, CIA Agent David Edwards had just been handed a packet marked: *Top Priority*.

A few minutes later, he got a telephone call with a stern verbal order: "Agent Edwards, I'm putting you in charge of the entire Western district, North and South. They are sure to hit the west coast next. Find these goddamned terrorists, Edwards. And I mean find them, now!"

Those succinct and inflexible words had come from the Director of the CIA himself, in Washington, D. C. This was being treated as an international incident, so the CIA had forward clearance on the investigation. The Director gave Edwards this ambiguous promotion with the definite task of coordinating all of the offices in the Rocky Mountain and Western Districts, with special emphasis on his own office in Los Angeles.

Every security bureau in the world was alerted to find this terrorist organization.

Edwards had a copy of the first "warning" press release and the summary press release from the terrorists, a memo from AP&G Oil Company and some jpeg photos and reports of the damage. This was all the information that was currently available. He laid the papers on a table in front of a big wall map of North America with a solitary pin in Texas.

Edwards and his team began the almost impossible task of trying to piece the scant information together. "Okay, here's what we know, which is not a lot. In the middle of the night, the AP&G Oil Company facility in southeastern Texas was blown up. Two people were injured during the explosions. Neither seriously, but the physical destruction of the plant was total. We don't know who did it. We don't know exactly why they did it. They're domestic, or so they say. They call themselves 'eco-terrorists.' We don't know how they did it. We don't know if this was just a single instance, or whether they have plans to do more damage. Their public communication says, 'Expect More'. Where and when, who knows? Any ideas?"

One of the agents looking at the photos answered Edwards. "Lot of damage down there. To do this much destruction, they'd have to have gone into the refinery in advance and planted some pretty sophisticated explosives. We're checking the employee logs and what's left of their security camera footage to see if the same people were at work during the week, or if there were any new people. I'll report the findings."

Edwards spoke. "Yes, yes, keep on that angle.

Another agent jumped in. "The memo from AP&G Oil states that most of their gasoline and petrochemicals have been contaminated and neutralized. We don't know how the terrorists might have done this, but our lab people are working on it now."

Edwards, more frustrated, started pushing them. "Look people, there are still a lot of unanswered questions. They say they aren't foreign terrorists. But, is that true? Any groups out there boasting that they did the job? Find out if there are any declarations. Are they an isolated group? Or, are they part of a larger organization? Can we find out any of their plans? Are they funded? And if so, by whom? Somebody get on that angle. Look, use every one of your undercover people, whether they're with the Company, or paid informants. We've got to get more info, and we need to get it fast."

To himself he said. "Damn, even Sherlock Holmes needed clues."

Edwards had no idea that Eric and Clay were the ringleaders he was looking for. If he'd known that fact, it would have only made him even more frustrated and crazy.

Another bulletin announced that the "eco-terrorists" would strike again. As usual, where or when was omitted in the release.

Saya arrived in Denver and again rented a van, then picked up Clay and Eric at the designated location. The same blindfolding procedure was followed to ensure total security. Clay then drove to pick up the others.

With the team gathered, they drove to a little warehouse located in the suburbs of Denver. At exactly nine o'clock in the evening, Eric opened the overhead door and Clay backed the van inside.

The case of equipment was there as usual. They all huddled around Eric and Clay to learn how this new operation would work.

Eric told them the plan. "This one is a bit different. We are going to kill and contaminate about 2,000 head of live cattle and then destroy the slaughterhouse and packing facility, then contaminate all the hanging and boxed beef inside the buildings. Our target location is the Mammoth Beef operation about 35 miles southwest of Denver. Mammoth Meat Company is America's biggest beef lot and packing house. They are selling 4-D beef, that's an animal that is Dead, Dying, Diseased or Down. They mix that flesh in with the good stuff. To them it's cost effective. No waste. The production line never stops, even if someone gets caught in the line or is injured. Workers have been maimed and killed and OSHA has cited them many times, too.

"Jesus..." Even Clay was disgusted by this litany of violations.

"Cattle feces and manure have been regularly found in their meat boxes. They've distributed beef that has active e.coli and salmonella. Most of that meat was consumed by humans. Deaths and sickness have occurred."

Clay piped up. "These bastards ruin the idea of a good hamburger or steak."

Eric continued. "The EPA has also cited them for uncontrolled run-off from their feedlot. This condition has gone on for years with no correction. It's ruining a huge mountain aquifer. The water is becoming toxic. This corporation has no conscience and only looks at the bottom line. These people at Mammoth Beef have been busted time after time by the EPA and USDA for health and food product hazards."

Clay took over, now. "So tonight, we're going to make their stockholders and bean counters go crazy. It's a total wipe-out, people. Tomorrow, Mammoth Beef will not exist."

The heavy container was loaded into the van. Eric gathered them around explaining the details.

After careful study of the map, they had some serious discussion about each of their roles in this new operation.

Then the team got in the van. Four of them lay on the floor with the container crate and were covered by blankets.

Clay drove a short distance and entered the Interstate highway heading south toward the target.

It was a cool and cloudy night in Colorado. The bright moon hiding behind the cloud cover made it very dark. Perfect conditions for their clandestine operation.

As usual, Ian and George were dropped closest to the target and George began to destroy the electronics at the site, while Ian surveyed.

Ian called to the firebase to launch the warning drones.

The WHITE drones exploded in the night air and screamed their message in several foreign languages:

Bombs have been placed in every building. Poison gas will explode. If you stay it will kill you. Explosions will begin in two minutes. Evacuate the buildings now. Get far away from the buildings and feedlots. At least 300 feet. Hurry. You must leave now. Run for your lives. You have no time left!

The message repeated as the workers on the night shift began to leave the buildings, stumbling over each other, running wildly for cover. They were in a panic.

Ian gave the all clear signal, and Clay ordered Jake to fire a RED drone. Pandemonium! A building burst into flames.

Clay ordered the launch of the GREEN drone.

The GREEN toxic missiles were set to explode at about fifteen feet above the cattle in the feedlot.

At the loud sounds of the overhead explosions, the livestock started to stampede, and then suddenly they stopped, and began to fall over.

The lethal gas was spreading in every direction.

The cattle were dropping like flies and the gurgling and gasping sounds mixed with their eerie groaning could be heard by Ian and George who were nearly half a mile away.

Then, there was silence in the night.

Clay ordered two more GREEN drones launched and directed Jake to penetrate the packing plant.

They could see the flashes through the window as the poisonous projectile exploded inside.

The GREEN drones were followed by the RED missiles causing big explosions and incendiary fires.

The offices were destroyed. The slaughter operations were on fire, and all of the cattle were dead.

Through his binoculars Eric stared, transfixed, at the carnage of hundreds of dead cattle and the building of fire.

They all sat for a moment until the wail of police, fire and ambulance sirens jolted them back to reality.

This mission was completed.

Hurriedly, they put all of the equipment back into the container, sprayed the "juice," got in the van, and departed. Another major violator was put out of business.

A summary of the raid and its destruction was released and appeared in every paper and TV news report:

Last night, the operating facilities of the Mammoth Meat facilities in Denver, Colorado were destroyed. Mammoth Meat was a major and habitual ecological violator and has been cited many times by OSHA, EPA, FDA and USDA. Mammoth Beef had done nothing to correct the pollution caused by their feedlot run-off or to cure the health violations of their slaughter processes, meatpacking operations or their products. Therefore, since Mammoth Meat has not complied with the EPA, we, as citizens, have undertaken to severely penalize them. Mammoth Meat is out of business. It has been destroyed. We have also contaminated their beef products, therefore making all products unusable and toxic.

WARNING: Do not consume any Mammoth Meat products for they will make you sick and possibly cause death. If our government will not stop the widespread poisoning of our food chain and the pollution by the big food corporations, we will. Our intentions are to strike again.

To tackle this terrorist problem, a combined meeting of the NSA, CIA and FBI was called.

The orders came from the President, himself: The orders were clear:

There is to be no conflict between the investigative agencies. Each will share what is known about this serious situation. Suggestions will be made by each agency. Each agency is to move forward, on its own, in pursuit of the terrorists and will continue to share all information they gather with the other agencies. I am going to Congress to have them appoint an investigative oversight committee for this unusual situation.

And, in one of the rare non-partisan political moments in history, Congress unanimously approved this committee.

It seemed like a sensible plan. This fact-finding oversight committee and the national defense agencies had the same information. However, the facts were still sketchy. Who the terrorists were, where and when they would strike again, was a mystery. None of them really knew anything. The greatest minds in world of security were baffled.

The media was on the case and the people of this country and the world knew of the results of the eco-terrorists.

All of the national news bureaus had opinions, but they had no more facts than the government agencies. The media, as usual, caused alarm with their wild speculations, blasting the government for doing nothing.

Returning from the joint meeting in Washington to LA, Agent G. David Edwards called his top men in to report. Frustrated, he launched right in. "My superiors are on my ass, and so are the FBI, NSA, and Joint Chiefs—top brass of government. Somehow, some way, we have to solve this thing. Okay, let's look at what we know. First, a Texas oil refinery and now, in Denver, they've hit a meat packing operation. What do they want? What's next?"

One of the agents spoke up. "We do know this: all evidence is destroyed each time. Same M.O. used in Texas and in Denver."

Another agent offered, "Our forensics people have never seen anything like this. All that's left at the crime scene is a mass of goo. Our guys don't even know what kind of acid or what chemical is being used. No evidence of any kind, so we don't know what types of materiel they are employing.

Edwards didn't find any of this helpful. "Are they using mortars? Or have they planted explosives in advance in the buildings? How did they kill all those cattle? How did they contaminate all the meat products?"

A third agent read from a report. "Sir, our forensic people have determined from an autopsy of the cattle that were killed by a form of Serin gas."

Edwards was incensed. "Serin gas? How did these guys get a hold of an outlawed poison?"

The third agent continued. "Yeah, and further, our people have ex-amined the rubble and discovered that the explosions were caused by an 'unknown' explosive containing traces of thermite."

Edwards was not happy. "Unknown explosive? Thermite?"

The second agent piped up. "These terrorists are serious as shit."

The first agent joined in. "And well-funded!"

Edwards stood up. "All I get from you people are the obvious facts. Masters of the obvious, all of you! It's like a bad homicide case with no clues. We're the CIA, boys. Not the LAPD or the FBI. I get that these corporations and their operations are effectively 'dead,' murdered. And we haven't got a clue what their weapons are... We don't know who, or when or where they'll strike again. We do know that they are highly organized. We think they are using military tactical weapons. Where will they hit next? What are their goals? What kind of group is this? Is it the same group or a separate group? How do they get to their target loca-tions? Planes, trains? Do they steal cars or rent them? Why are the hits always outside, but not too far from, major cities?"

The second agent interrupted. "Yeah, we can check the stolen car lists. Check the car and truck rentals. Check the airlines. Check the..."

Edwards pounded on his desk. "Jesus, we don't even have a descrip-tion of who we're looking for. Get me some evidence! Get me suspects!"

Edwards stood up straight and took a deep breath, trying to calm him-self. He adjusted his tie and sat back down behind his desk. "People, this is not an impossible task. There are always mistakes to be uncovered."

A clerk knocked at Edwards office door and rushed in, handing him a sheet of paper. "Sir, we just received this. It's another 'announcement' from the eco-terrorists, but it doesn't say where or when they're going to strike."

Edwards grabbed the paper and jumped up from his desk, shouting at the assembled agents." Go do your damned jobs!"

The agents scattered out of Edwards office as he flopped back into his chair, head in his hands.

The next target was South Land Power & Light, the big coal-fired electric generation plant in southeastern Georgia.

Billy ordered Bob Scully to penetrate the computers of SLP&L. This time the computers would send statements to SLP&L customers with the following announcement just as Eric and Clay's team finished their next attack.

> *Dear Customer—Until SLP&L can provide you with clean-coal non-polluting electric energy you will not be charged further for your electric service. This clean-up may take months. Enjoy your FREE electric.—Thank You.*

Eric's plan: Cripple. Disable. Destroy. Billy's plan: Embarrass. Ruin reputations. Cause lost revenue.

Together they were very effective.

Saya was again instructed to rent a van. The following morning, she picked up Eric and Clay.

After getting the other team members on board they went to a warehouse in Macon, Georgia, about 85 miles south of Atlanta and just a few miles from the target. Billy's people had rented a small warehouse building and delivered the equipment crate for the next job. Every detail had been thought out, ensuring no delay between attacks and smooth operations.

With the group assembled at the warehouse, Eric spoke first. "This particular electric generation plant owned by SLP&L has been cited by the EPA for air emissions of SO_2 and CO_2 far beyond acceptable limits and unbelievably high levels of mercury. In addition, the owners SLP&L have been notified by the EPA that their coal-ash slurry pond is leaking toxic chemicals into the aquifer. The pond is considered inadequately constructed and not safe. It could burst open at any time.

Clay added, "Coal ash contains toxic materials like lead, arsenic, selenium and thallium and such sites contaminate the air, drinking water and surface water."

Eric continued. "This huge coal burning facility is the largest single source of carbon dioxide emissions in the United States."

Clay took over. "There are six turbines in the plant. It's capable of producing 900,000 kilowatts of electricity. That's enough to provide electricity for nearly 200,000 homes. The generating station runs twenty-four hours a day, but when electric demand is low during the night, the six turbines alternate, using only two turbines at a time."

Clay rolled out a map. "We attack at night. At 1:00 a.m. This job will be a little different from the refinery. The plan is to destroy only two turbine generators. This is a get-in-get-out operation. Our team will be assembled in a line on this hill less than a half a mile from the big generating station. We'll have a good view of the target and a clear visual of the operation for all of us."

As usual, George, the DEWEMP man, launched first, knocking out the communications systems at the plant. When George was satisfied that all communication systems were inoperable, he signaled Ian for an all-clear.

Jake got the go-head from Ian, and Clay ordered the launch of two of the WHITE warning shells for aerial release.

The WHITE drones deployed.

The warning message this time instructed all personnel to go to their cars and trucks in the parking lot and get as far away from the buildings as possible because there were bombs inside.

George targeted each of the vehicles with the DEWEMP systemically rendering all of the cars and trucks in the parking lot inoperable. No one could leave.

Eric wanted the workers to witness this destruction.

Ian scanned the area and saw the workers running to their vehicles. He sent his "all clear" to Jake. Clay ordered the firing of the RED drones.

The RED drones did the real work. The diesel fuel tanks ignited. The huge transformers in the substation were ablaze. A down-the-shaft hit on the cooling towers caused them to explode, and in an accidental hit the mountain of raw coal was set afire.

Everywhere there was twisted steel. The flames were huge and the destruction and confusion were rampant.

Suddenly, the powerhouse exploded with a tremendous roar followed by three more explosions. The roof of the great turbine building was blown off and the walls crumbled and began to fall.

The generation of electricity abruptly stopped.

Once the walls and roof had been blown away, Jake could see the targeted turbine generators. Now a special PURPLE drone was launched. This one was filled with the destructive "Gertz Juice." This would begin to melt the steel turbine. To make certain the huge turbine generators were completely destroyed, another PURPLE drone was launched and sent toward the targeted generators.

The powerhouse destruction was the signal for them to stop, destroy their equipment and get ready to exit.

Ian could see the workmen trying to start their engines. Some of them just stood and stared, awe struck, as the destruction continued.

It was time to leave. The equipment was demolished in the usual way and the team quickly got into their van.

They were safe and rolling down the road on their planned escape route, a two-lane country road chosen in order to avoid the rescue, police and fire vehicles, but still get them to the interstate as quickly as possible.

Suddenly, a local sheriff's car pulled out, flashing its emergency lights.

Saya pulled over.

Clay, in the front seat, said. "I'll handle this."

Saya got out on the driver's side.

Clay got out, too.

The officer walked over to Saya. "What's the hurry, honey? Big fire back there. Ya see it? Did ya get scared? Let's see your ID?"

The deputy took Saya's ID from her hand, looking her in the eye, then glancing at the ID. He looked over at Clay. "Where you comin' from, son, and where ya goin?"

Clay said in a southern drawl. "Lady's looking ta buy some of y'ur beautiful Georgia property, Sheriff. I'm Todd Browning, her real estate agent. And this is Miss Monica."

"Hmm. Awful strange time a night to take a look see at property, honey." The deputy looked lasciviously at Saya, and down at Saya's driver's license.

Clay walked behind the deputy and calmly plunged a knife into the base of his skull.

The deputy slumped to the ground.

Clay motioned Saya to get back in the van.

Eric jumped out.

Clay said, "Collateral damage."

Eric nodded.

Eric and Clay dragged the dead deputy to the patrol car and put him in the front seat. Clay pulled the CB radio off the dashboard and smashed it.

Clay opened the gas tank, started the car and maneuvered it back to the middle of the road. Placing the dead man's feet lightly on the accelerator, Clay reached inside, put the patrol car in gear and pushed the deputy's body forward and quickly jumped back. The car took off like a bullet, ran down the road and off into a tree, bursting into flames.

Eric and Clay ran back to the van and jumped inside. Clay blithely said, "One cop down, goal to go."

Soon they were heading north on I-75 toward Atlanta.

Their exit plan was the same. Saya dropped each of them off at bus stops near their hotels and returned the van to the airport after-hours lot.

That night they all slept knowing they had again done something good for mankind.

And, Billy slept like a baby.

The next day, a summary of the operation was released:

Last night we destroyed most of the operating facilities of SLP&L which was a dirty coal-fired electric production plant located in Hodges Grove, Georgia. SLP&L is a major and habitual ecological violator, cited many times by EPA. SLP&L has done nothing to correct the burning of dirty coal and the ensuing pollution to the atmosphere, air and water aquifers. Therefore, since they have not complied with the EPA, we as citizens, have undertaken to severely penalize them. Today, the number four and number five turbine generators, as well the buildings, storage and cooling facilities of SLP&L have been destroyed. If our government will not stop the widespread pollution by the dirty-coal-burning electric generation industry, we will! Expect more destruction of the coal-fired electric industry!

Soon another warning email was sent to all media, corporations and government agencies.

The terrorists would attack again.

But, this time it was a ruse.

Billy, Eric and Clay wanted to observe what the reaction would be and learn what the government might do to stop them.

Eighteen

Hurricane House

This last strike had hit a nerve. The electric generation industry had a lot of clout and, combined with the coal mine owners, they raised a big stink in Washington.

Again, the media attacked the government for doing nothing. They reported the people's demand for it to stop.

Congress was up in arms, insistent that the NSA, FBI and CIA together bring a close to the terrorist activities. Congress not only wanted it to stop, they wanted blood!

Billy was not troubled by the news. He'd planned a little vacation for Eric, Clay and their people at his *Hurricane House* on the Gulf of Mexico.

Still on schedule, Clay called his team in the morning. He told them each to buy tickets on the Amtrak train to New Orleans leaving the next day from Atlanta. Four of them bought tickets at separate travel agents and Eric and Clay bought their tickets at the train station.

The next day, they were all were onboard the historic *Crescent* for New Orleans. Soon they would taste a bit of Billy's southern hospitality. They passed each other on the train without giving the other notice. The train ride was long, but relaxing.

Upon arrival in New Orleans, in groups of two, they took separate taxis to different hotels. They didn't check in at the hotels, but waited out front. Soon they were met by one of Billy's men who took them in private cars to Billy's mansion, *Hurricane House*.

Eric and Clay were dropped at the front door of the huge mansion. Even these two worldly men were impressed. Billy's *Hurricane House* exceeded anyone's imagined dream house. It was magnificent.

Inside, there were sixty-five sleeping rooms, an immense dining room, an indoor-outdoor swimming pool, a freshwater trout stream and a saltwater lagoon, each filled with fish and crustaceans for the dinner table. Huge hydroponic gardens grew all of the vegetables and herbs used at *Hurricane House*. The electricity was totally provided by solar, wind and tidal-driven hydroelectric power. Billy's *Hurricane House* was completely self-sufficient.

Some distance away from the main house there were barns for cows, pigs and poultry, all naturally fed, providing the freshest meat, eggs and dairy products for the guests.

In another building was an industrial style meat and vegetable processing room for the huge commercial-sized kitchen. All of the chefs and cooking staff in service rivaled those in any five-star hotel.

Hurricane House's general amusement area had everything. A billiards room, bowling alley, a card and chess room, a ping-pong and air hockey room, an indoor rifle and handgun range, and an archery range, all of which guaranteed plenty of fun, even in bad weather.

The music and movie room was outfitted with comfortable theater-style seats for listening to favorite music tracks or watching movies. The custom-designed chairs were tall-backed, plush affairs with unique little tables and built-in audio/video controls and stereo speakers in the headrest.

The bar in this room served any drink one might call for and the snacks were top-notch quality. If you couldn't find something to eat, drink, or do at *Hurricane House*, then you really weren't trying at all.

Eric and Clay were relaxing at the indoor pool, sipping glasses of scotch, when Rob Collings approached Eric.

"Got some bad news for you Eric. Your friend Fred Masinga is dead. They say he had a heart attack."

"Are you kidding me? Freddy can't be dead. What the hell is going on, Rob?"

"Did Freddy have a bad heart, Eric?"

"Well, yeah. But it was under control. And he knew his limits. That's why he just wanted to be behind the scenes… Are you sure, man?"

Clay chimed in. "CIA can get rough. Their version of interrogation is not exactly square with the Geneva Convention, if you get my drift… Awfully coincidental, don't you think, Rob? First Elaine, now Freddy."

Rob stood in silence.

Eric sat with his head in his hands.

Clay stood up, grabbed his and Eric's glasses and refilled them at the poolside bar. "But you know, Rob, there are no coincidences when the CIA is involved.

Eric remembered Freddy's description of meeting with CIA Agent Edwards. Eric felt alternately defeated and furious. "Edwards…I'm gonna kill that bastard!"

Rob calmly responded. "Eric, I'll continue looking into it for you."

Two weeks had elapsed since the last incident. Nothing had happened anywhere. Agent Edwards still had no clue who the terrorists might be or how they operated or even their true intentions. He was hopeful that maybe the destruction was all over.

But the attack missions were far from over. Soon, another warning message was issued. This time with a date.

*On **January 15**, we will attack and destroy the offices and all operations at one of the companies who have been con-*

tinually cited by the EPA, FDA, USDA as major and ha-
bitual environmental polluters.

WE ARE AMERICANS! (Not foreign terrorists) We are U.S.
citizens who are fed-up with the poisoning of our environ-
ment. We will tolerate no more. We are angry. We are many.
We intend to put these serial violators out of business. You
have been warned.

As usual, the message didn't disclose any particular location, but now, the date of the next attack was revealed. This warning caused great fear and confusion for the government, law enforcement agencies, as well as all North American corporations.

This time Eric focused on factory farming. He knew about the industrial production of chickens and turkeys that were being fed with massive amounts of antibiotics and growth hormones to keep them alive in conditions that would otherwise kill the animals.

The human autoimmune system was being damaged, too. This reckless use of antibiotics injected into the poultry reduced the efficacy of many drugs used for treating humans by speeding up the development of drug-resistant bacteria. Along with other chemicals and substances, like the arsenic-laden feed additives used to increase weight gain in the poultry, people were slowly being poisoned without knowing it. Apparently, these producers of food were only interested in producing more profits and had no concern for the health of the consumers of their products.

In addition, in order to speed up the processing lines, visual inspection was no longer used. In its place, the poultry were bathed constantly in a shower of disinfectant that contained chlorine and peracetic acid. Not only were the workers inhaling the fumes, getting sick and dying, but there was some evidence that theses substances remained in the flesh of the poultry ultimately ingested by humans.

Eric was convinced that an immediate and powerful message must be sent to the poultry industry. The plan was to target *Tasty Good Chickens*, one of the largest poultry producers in the world. TGC was located in a rural area of Connecticut. This attack would do to this poultry polluter what they'd done to the Mammoth Beef operation.

The strategy was basically the same as was used in the Denver attack. Kill all of the chickens and turkeys, then in a poisonous way, make their corpses unfit for consumption by humans or as feed for animals. Then blow up the slaughter and packing facilities.

The team met in Hartford and followed the standard procedures. In a storage building in the suburbs, they found the equipment container, surveyed the maps and settled on their plan of attack.

Since the poultry operation was located on vast barren farmland, mortars were the weapons of choice.

First, George destroyed the communications and vehicles with his DEWEMP gun. Then Jake fired WHITE parachuted missiles with the audio warnings. The night shift crew fearfully ran away from the buildings.

Next, the needle-pointed GREEN poison gas missiles were sent in to quickly destroy the living poultry. Then the RED incendiary rounds launched setting the buildings aflame and destroying the freezers and processing equipment.

All proceeded on schedule and according to plan. Their mission was again a success. The facilities of the offending *Tasty Good Chickens* had been totally destroyed.

To aid the final ruination of this offending company, Billy's computer specialists successfully hacked and corrupted the internal CPUs of the mainframes at the New York and Connecticut offices of *Tasty Good Chickens*.

As a final blow, Billy destroyed the computer systems of all of TGC's distributors and wholesalers.

The synopsis to the media of their mission was standard:

Last night we destroyed all of the operating facilities of Tasty Good Chicken in Hartford, Connecticut. Known as TGC, Inc., the corporation had been a major and habitual violator and has been cited many times by EPA, OSHA, FDA and USDA. TGC, Inc. has not complied with the EPA, OSHA, FDA and USDA orders to immediately remove the antibiotics and growth hormones fed to their poultry and improve the growing conditions. These additives have been proven to harm humans.

Today, we have executed our own penalty on TGC, Inc. Their operations have been destroyed and all of their chicken and turkey products have been chemically contaminated. WARNING: The public is hereby advised not to eat any Tasty Good Chicken products. Consuming these products will cause illness and possible death. If our government will not stop the widespread polluting, adulterating and poisoning of our foodstuffs, we will. Our intentions are to continue destructive actions!

With this release, Billy blasted out some creative writing to the government, corporations and the media, stoking public support with glamorous Jesse James-folk-here-like descriptions of the excitement and pathos of the team's missions. These fabricated accounts underscored the idea that this eco-terrorist group was unstoppable and that they would strike again and again until the government and the corporations made the necessary changes the group demanded of them.

Billy expected the general population to side quickly with the eco-terrorists.

The next day TV, radio, newspapers and the emerging internet news feeds were brimming with expansive articles based on Billy's made-up stories.

The public outcry rallying behind the eco-terrorists caused every state governor and U.S. Congressman and Senator to hear from their constituents in a very raucous and unusual manner.

Billy was correct in his assumption of positive public reaction. Poll after poll showed that the citizens didn't want the eco-terrorists to stop their destructive actions. People considered the eco-terrorists modern super-heroes, helping humanity. The public supported them in demanding that the corporations correct their ways, obey regulations and stop polluting.

Eric and Clay were beside themselves with joy. They were making history and slowly causing the status quo to change.

Conversely, law enforcement, who never give up, and rarely close a file, especially one of this magnitude, remained trapped in box they still couldn't define. The CIA, FBI, and NSA joined together to organize all law enforcement departments, local police and sheriffs across the U.S. in order to catch these criminals.

Edwards had a hunch that there had to be a single vehicle, like a truck or a van, that the eco-terrorists traveled together in, to and away from each attack site. He thought it was unlikely they'd continued to use the same vehicle. They couldn't get it to the next location fast enough. That meant the vehicles were rented. Edwards had the CIA put out a bulletin to the new U.P.A., the United Police Agencies, to check all trucks and vans that had been rented prior to the terrorist attacks in the big cities near the hits: Houston, Denver, Atlanta and Hartford.

With this concerted effort, they began to make some headway. After laboriously reviewing CCTV footage, there seemed to be a woman of similar build, but varying hair colors/styles and names renting a van at airports in each of the designated cities within 48 hours of each hit. Edwards did not think this was a coincidence. Edwards had his team create a composite of the the four "appearances" and had agents send it to all car rental offices in all cities in North America. They were to be on the lookout for this woman. If seen, they were instructed to contact the CIA immediately.

Within a day, the results of the search paid off. Saya was spotted renting a van at the Los Angeles International airport.

Edwards contacted the car rental office for the local address she provided. It was a phony. No such place existed.

A local APB was issued for the suspect vehicle. It wasn't long before the LA police intercepted the car. Saya was taken into custody.

As ordered, the CIA was notified.

David Edwards was excited. This was the first break he'd gotten on this case. He wasn't going to waste the opportunity.

He ordered one of his men to pick up the suspect from the LA police station and bring her back to a little storeroom in East LA that the CIA sometimes used for interrogations.

Edwards grilled the blindfolded Saya mercilessly. "Okay, we know you're a key part of this eco-terrorist organization. You've rented vehicles in Houston, Denver, Atlanta and last week in Hartford. In each of these areas very nasty things happened. You and your group were responsible. No use denying it. Now who are the leaders? What's your next target? We know you rented a van in LA today. What's the location of the next hit?"

Saya was tied to a chair. "I know you won't believe me, but I don't know who they are or where the next target is. I only know them as Number One and Number Two. They contact me. They only tell me what to do just before I'm supposed to do it, and nothing more."

Edwards didn't like her answer. After smacking her around, Saya was then water-boarded. She continued to deny having any knowledge of how the targets were planned and repeated that she didn't know who was in charge or where the next target was. She was telling him the truth.

Saya screamed, gasping for air. "I haven't been told yet. Only Number One and Number Two know the details. Please stop. Please stop…"

Edwards kept up the water torture, demanding that she identify the names of Number One and Number Two and how they operated. In fact, Saya couldn't tell him because she didn't know their real names.

But Edwards didn't believe her.

She kept repeating. "They're just Number One and Number Two. That's all I know. Please stop. Oh, not again! Stoooopp…"

Saya had to save her life. She'd been trained for an occasion like this. Finally, she apparently broke. "Stop…you're killing me! Okay, okay, you win. I'm supposed to pick up Number One and Number Two at 8:00 a.m. tomorrow morning at the Starlight Motel on La Brea, and then I'll get my orders."

She knew that if anyone other than herself were in that car, Number One and Number Two would know what to do.

But Edwards was not convinced. He wanted more details. He was sure she had more to give. Again and again they used the torture. Cruelly, he persisted and one too many times the water was poured on her face and down her throat. It was too much. Agonizingly, Saya died from the water-boarding.

Edwards had destroyed the only source of evidence in the case. He was momentarily shaken. Regaining his composure, he ordered her body to be taken north of Hollywood to the Silver Lake reservoir and dumped. If, or when, she was found it would look like a simple drowning. No one knew she existed, yet. He was sure he had some time to pull something together.

Edwards paced the room as the agents cleaned up. He instructed everyone, including those dumping the body, that this was a silent operation. No leaks. No discussion.

He had to think. Finally, he decided that they would use Saya's rented van and suit up a female agent to drive and make the planned pick-up the next morning. Edwards and another agent would hide on the floor in the back. He was confident that they would quickly and efficiently arrest Number One and Number Two as soon as they got into the van. Simple.

Agent Edwards wondered about the identities Number One and Number Two and whether they were the masterminds behind these terrorist attacks, or just flunkies like the dead girl being packaging up in front of him. Why were they doing all this? What was the real motive?

Edwards was sure that when he got hold of those two, no matter what he would have to do, he'd make them talk, but he'd be more careful. Keep them alive. And that would make up for this sloppy mistake. He wasn't going to call for backup in the morning. He was going to bust this case, himself.

The next morning Edwards and his agents drove to the rendezvous location. The van arrived at the pick up address. It was a shabby motel and not in a good part of the city. It was 8:00 a.m. They were on time.

The Saya-look-alike sat in the driver's seat and the agents were on the floor in the back of the van.

Just as Saya had told Edwards, two men appeared. They approached the van one on either side, opening the side doors of the van. The driver and the other agent rolled out on either side of the van and, after a brief scuffle, the agents subdued and handcuffed the two men.

When they were put into the van, Edwards was astounded to see Clay Perkins and Eric Atkins. "Well, well, well. The dead do return. I would have never figured it out. Good job. You had me guessing."

To the girl driver Edwards ordered. "Back to the storeroom and step on it."

"Once I get you two inside I'm going to find out everything. You'll talk just like that Israeli girl talked."

Eric and Clay looked knowingly at one another.

Shortly, they arrived at the hidden CIA site. Clay and Eric were roughly handled and taken into the barren room that held only some chairs and the table for the water-boarding in the center of the room under a fluorescent light.

"First you, Clay. You have to be the brains of this outfit. You there, help me put him on the table."

An opportunity had arisen. Clay head-butted Edwards to the floor and then wheel-kicked the other agent. Edwards and the agent were unconscious.

The female agent shouted for Clay to stop and drew her gun.

Eric took his cue and, even though he was cuffed to a chair, he swung it around wildly, knocking the female agent off-balance and to the floor.

Clay finished her off using his foot to stomp her neck.

Lots of noise, but in east LA no one noticed or cared.

Eric said, "I can just reach this guy. I'll search him." Struggling blindly, he finally yanked the handcuff keys free. "Okay, okay. I've got 'em."

Clay responded. "Quick, unlock these damned things" Clay knelt down with his back to Eric who clumsily unlocked the handcuffs. Clay grabbed the keys and unlocked Eric's cuffs, and said, "I'll get their guns."

Eric pulled his hands free and loosened the bindings holding his legs to the chair.

Clay removed the automatic pistols from Edwards and the other agents. Clay handed Eric one and kept two for himself.

With the CIA agents down, the situation was reversed. Eric and Clay had captured G. David Edwards. Edwards regained consciousness and staggered to his feet. He noticed the guns pointing at him.

Eric demanded, "So. Tell me about my wife. How'd you kill her? What really happened?"

Eric shoved Edwards. "And what about Freddy. Did you kill him, too?"

Edwards smiled and boasted, adding further insult. "Yes. I killed both of your women and Freddy, too. Your wife was an accident. Your Israeli girl and Freddy were just too weak. They just couldn't answer my questions."

Eric was enraged. "You murderer!"

Edwards was calm. "Oh, yes, oh yes. I'm a brutal murderer. Just like your friend Clay. That's how we were trained, weren't we? Company men. Although, it seems Clay couldn't do his job. I ordered you to make the hit on Eric, Clay, you fucking traitor…"

Edwards was startled as Clay systematically put several bullets into each of the unconscious agents. Edwards was stunned at the coolness of Clay's action. "That was not necessary, Clay. It won't do you any good. The Company will still win. We always do."

Eric waved a gun in Edward's face and talked loudly. "You bastard, I should kill you right here and now!"

"Go ahead and do it, you coward."

Eric hesitated.

Clay plunged his combat knife deep into the back of David Edwards' neck. His airway compromised, Edwards fell to his knees, gurgling, and lurched forward flat onto the floor.

Clay pulled out his knife and rolled him over. Clay stood over him watching as the struggling Edwards' eyes bulged. With the precision of a surgeon, Clay knelt down, pinning Edwards' flailing arms and body and expertly cut off his head, throwing it into the corner. He picked up Edwards' bloody body and dropped it among the dead agents.

Clay said to Eric, who was in shock, "All this mess, the dead bodies and the M.O. will confuse the CIA investigative boys and stall the chase for a while. Remember, the Company never forgets, and never stops. Someone will continue to pursue us. It's not over, yet, buddy."

Nineteen

Dead in the Water

An ex-MI6 British intelligence officer, Carlton Pangborn, was appointed to lead the West Coast Office and more agents were added to the district. His MI6 training included how to recruit and handle informants, how to operate under a cover identity, and development of various tradecraft skills such as use of dead drops, surveillance and counter-surveillance techniques, secret writing and codes. Pangborn was scrupulously precise.

After the untimely death of Agent Edwards, Pangborn personally and thoroughly read Edwards' files. There was little to go on.

The developments related to Saya's capture and the subsequent encounter with Eric and Clay were, of course, not notated in Edward's files. He was killed before he could make a report. There was no reference on the day of his death about where he was going, or what he and his team were doing at that warehouse. Everyone involved was dead. So those facts remained unknown.

The forensic team reported that the murder scene offered no real clues. The hit resembled those of middle-eastern assassins. Without more to go on and no ongoing investigation to tie it to, the case was temporarily set aside.

Edwards' files came to a dead end. Pangborn was forced to start where Edwards files left off. He was no closer to finding the "eco-terrorists" than Edwards had been.

At their first meeting with their new boss, the CIA agents got direct and strong instructions from Pangborn.

"Gentlemen, I believe this was a guerrilla hit. Even though we have officially called the death of David Edwards and his team an act by middle-eastern operatives, I personally think it could be linked to our 'eco-terrorists.' Now, I understand that murder has not been their M.O. so far, but they may have been surprised and reacted impulsively. Regardless, this was murder, and we must find the perpetrators.

"The last entry in Agent Edwards file included some notes about Eric Atkins and former agent Clay Perkins, as well as Atkins' wife and a Freddy Masinga as suspects. Interestingly, these alleged suspects are all dead. I'm afraid Edwards was not on the right track. If we review Edwards' conclusions: Size of terrorist group? UNKNOWN. Location of terrorists? UNKNOWN. Reason for terrorist actions? UNKNOWN. Terrorists next target: UNKNOWN... Unknown! Unknown! Well now, that's about what we have to go on. We know nothing."

One of the agents spoke up. "It did seem that Agent Edwards was kind of chasing his tail. He had unknowns and no tangible suspicions. The investigations of the terrorists' crime scenes revealed no clues. The weaponry used was dissolved by some acid our science boys still can't identify..."

Pangborn interrupted. "Exactly. We have discovered naught. We know zero and are now left waiting for the other shoe to drop."

A clerk came in and handed Pangborn a sheet of paper. He read the memo to himself and then read it aloud to the others. "Here we go again. Another ambiguous warning from the terrorists. Same M.O. Doesn't say where, only when. Could be anywhere. It's a huge country. I suppose we are expected to just wait and hope that... Damn it all! We've got to figure this out. Without a break, it could go on indefinitely. Gentlemen, we are missing something; something obvious. I'm sure of it."

The planned raid at the big petrochemical plant in Los Angeles was put on hold. Rob and Billy thought it was too close to the scene of the murders and that the CIA would probably launch a full court press on Los Angeles.

They were right. The CIA was fully alerted and watching every potential target in the Los Angeles and Orange County areas.

But the next action would be far north of Los Angeles—The Pacific Fish & Seafood Company, an Asian-owned importer located in Seattle, Washington.

The plan was to destroy the warehouse building of PFSC and all of its contents, the ships on the docks, as well as the fleet of semi-trailers.

The PFSC main freezer storage warehouse was located just blocks away from the docks. It was huge, covering several acres. Hundreds of refrigerated semi-trailers waited to be loaded with the toxic cargo that would be delivered to groceries and restaurants in cities all across North America.

The freezer sections were housed in a flat-top building. It would take a lot of Gertz's PURPLE incendiary bombs to destroy the fish and seafood inside.

The cargo ships and semi-trailers, if hit correctly with the incendiary bombs, would ignite causing the entire bunch to end up as one mass of molten, twisted metal. The delivery system chosen for this job, again, was mortars.

Collins hadn't had a chance yet to train a new driver, since the unexpected death of Saya. Clay became the designated the driver.

The team assembled in a storage unit in downtown Seattle near the target.

Eric explained the mission. "PFSC has been a flagrant FDA violator. Without conscience or care for the law or the safety of consumers, they import tons of fish and seafood that the FDA has found are caught and kept in conditions that render it unfit for humans to eat. We know the

FDA only inspects 2% of imported fish and seafood. Over 80% of the fish and seafood we eat are imported. That's about 90 million tons just last year. Most of the imported seafood contains mercury, melamine, fungicides, bacteria and salmonella. These fish and seafood are raised in farms that are polluted with raw sewage and industrial waste. Because they are bred and raised in this filth, the pollutants end up in their flesh, and then we ingest it into our systems."

Clay picked up where Eric left off. "PFSC is a huge operation and even though they've be cited by the FDA, they continue to import products from Asia that would not pass federal inspection. How many people are sickened and killed each year from this one source can only be speculated. So, PFSC is our next target."

The team pulled the equipment from the crate and readied for the mission.

Eric reminded them all, "Our goal here remains the same: to alert our government that they need to genuinely protect the food that we consume."

So as not to alert the public or police, the usual parachute warning for evacuation was modified. Needle-pointed WHITE missiles entered through the roof and broadcast their warnings inside.

The workers were frightened and scattered as usual.

Then RED incendiary missiles fell through the roof as the firebombs rained down on the warehouse. Then Gertz's GREEN poison gas bombs launched to contaminate the insides of the processing plant.

The quadrants were changed on the second mortar to shell the cargo ships with RED bombs. One by one, the container ships were set afire. The last to be hit were the semi-trailers. This required two mortar locations and split-second coordination. Alternating PURPLE then RED shells decimated and melted the semi-trailers.

Elapsed time from beginning to end of the mission was less than eight minutes.

Everything was ablaze. The team dropped all the mortars and equipment into the 'Gertz-juice' and it quickly became a mass of ooze.

The team made their way out just as the fire and police arrived at the destroyed and blazing scene. Until the arson investigation completed, it would appear as though this was a huge industrial accident.

The hope was that this would allow the team to retreat to safer ground, unnoticed.

The general public followed the eco-terrorists' adventures just as generations ago the people followed the exploits of Robin Hood, Jesse James and John Dillinger. The public loved these new brave terrorists for fighting back against the big corporations. They were becoming folk heroes. Even though no one knew their names, the eco-terrorists were rapidly becoming super-stars.

As usual, the summary of the destruction of Pacific Fish and Seafood Company went out to the media.

Last night we destroyed all of the operating facilities of the Pacific Fish and Seafood Company in Seattle, Washington. Known as PFSC, Inc., they have been a major and habitual violator and cited many times by EPA, OSHA, FDA and USDA. PFSC, Inc. has not complied with the EPA, OSHA, FDA and USDA orders to immediately remove the antibiotics and growth hormones fed to their fish and seafood. These additives have been proven to harm humans. Today, we have executed our own penalty on PFSC, Inc. Their operations have been smashed and all of their fish and seafood products have been chemically contaminated.

WARNING: The public is hereby advised not to eat any PFSC, Inc. products. Consumption of this contaminated fish and seafood will cause illness and possible death. If our government will not stop the widespread polluting, adulterating and poisoning of our foodstuffs, we will. Our intention is to continue our actions!

Billy and his "computer devils," as he liked to call them, had done an exceptional job on their end. The computer team had contacted every customer from the data banks of PFSC, alerting them of the destruction of PFSC and how the FDA had turned a blind eye on the contaminated fish and seafood products of PFSC. They were warned that by distributing and serving poisoned products they had become accessories and eco-targets; they might face damage themselves.

Billy in his efficient fashion, communicated to all the importers as well as the Asian exporters, warning that what had happened to PFSC would happen to them if they didn't clean up their operations and provide safe food products.

Things were moving along just as Eric had planned. Clay was overjoyed because they were making fools of the CIA, the FBI and the government in general. Both of them liked being terrorists with a moral mission.

Soon, another warning message was sent out and the team prepared for their next mission. The usual warning communications were sent out without mentioning the location of the promised destruction.

In planning the strategic design for this next important mission, Rob Collings studied and adopted the methods allegedly used by the perpetrators of the riots and fire bombings of Los Angeles in 1992. In the riot aftermath, subsequent investigations by the authorities revealed that just four cars and eight people brought the entire fire, police and sheriff departments to their knees. After setting the fires, the fire departments were called in. When the firemen arrived, shots were fired at the firemen. The police were called to protect the firemen. Once the police were on the scene, the arsonists moved quickly to another site and repeated this same method. Quickly, all fire, police and sheriff departments were exhausted and had no more people or equipment available. Had not the National Guard been called in, the riots and arson would have continued indefinitely. The local media reported the perpetrators as "hit and run artists."

Collings decided to use similar tactics for this next operation. A military guerrilla-style action was planned. They would hit and run, too.

The auto industry was the next target: Detroit. The Motor City. The car capital of the world. It was to be an ingenious attack. The main target: the thousands of new cars that were housed in huge parking lots located across the city. They would destroy the "Big Three" inventories of cars, as they sat there all finished and ready for delivery.

In the afternoon, the team assembled. Eric addressed his band of loyalists. "Detroit makes the most cars in the world. They produce so many that they store them in lots awaiting delivery to their dealers. Internal combustion cars equal huge CO_2 emissions. Those emissions destroy the ozone layer, causing global warming. Cars should have zero emissions. All of the car companies are big investors in the oil companies. These industries are symbiotic. It takes oil and gasoline to run the cars. That profitable mutual association has been going on for a hundred years. The U.S. uses over one-third of all the gasoline in the world. Both industries know that the pollution caused by cars and diesel trucks adversely affects human health and the environment. Well, they need to wake up and make improvements in transportation. Electric cars are the only answer."

George asked, "But why destroy the cars?"

Clay answered. "Detroit needs to feel a sudden and big loss of profits and get some bad PR, too, in order to 'inspire' them to redesign their vehicles and get out of bed with Big Oil. Our statement to the media will explain why we did it. It should be shocking to the world, and anyhow, it's about time the people refused to buy any car that isn't all electric."

They opened their supply crate and discussed the instructions for the mission that would begin that evening.

For the first time, the "Gertz Juice" would be used as an offensive weapon. The plan was to employ special aerial mortar shells that would explode over the lots and disperse the acid-like "Juice" destroying the cars completely.

It was a dark night. No moonlight at all. The attack was planned for nighttime to prevent any civilians being injured.

Several "Juice" shells were launched first at the finished cars in the holding lots. Then, to ensure that the fire department and police would appear, time-delayed explosive shells and incendiary shells were fired to the main auto plants.

That accomplished, they moved on to the next site.

The "Gertz Juice" was working well. They hit four quadrants of the lot so that the disbursement was complete. Some of the shells were a little off and the steel cyclone fencing enclosing the lots was melted along with the cars.

That night all of the targeted locations were hit. Thousands of brand new cars were reduced to pools of goo.

The sky in Detroit erupted with one blaze after another. The shrieking sirens of the fire and police seemed to come from everywhere at once.

Billy, Eric and Clay had made their point by striking the auto industry, the heart of the American dream. Again, another media statement was released.

> *Last night, in Detroit, Michigan, we destroyed thousands of new cars built by the "Big Three" and their assembly plants. The internal combustion engines in these cars which burn gasoline send tons of SO^4 & CO^2 into our atmosphere each day. The auto industry and the oil industry are one. Even though the use of petro-fuels has been proven to cause lung diseases and cancers these industries will not stop. They don't care. The auto industry could have decided to make inexpensive, non-polluting, electric cars decades ago. Because they are heavily invested in the oil companies, and vice versa, they have chosen to go on pro-*

ducing the very expensive internal combustion cars. They make money both ways. Burning of gasoline is killing our planet, the ozone layer and the people. STOP BUYING internal combustion cars. DEMAND ELECTRIC CARS from the "Big Three." If our government will not stop these evil, polluting, uncaring companies, we will. Expect more!

In addition to the physical destruction, Billy's "computer devils" sent out a separate message to all of the North American "Big Three" car dealerships stating:

Car Dealers—*Thousands of your internal combustion cars are now destroyed. Before you replace them with more polluters, consider demanding that your auto manufacturer build all electric cars. If they don't, as fast as they make those gas buggies, we'll destroy them and their facilities. You will have nothing to sell. You will be out of business.*

Billy was satisfied with the air of drama at the end of this communication. He enjoyed stirring up a bit of confusion. The computers of these major corporations and their retail dealers were notified, and hopefully this would result in lost profits for the "Big Three."

The "eco-terrorists" were gaining not only public awareness, but increasing public approval.

After the Detroit mission, Eric thought about what they had done and the targets that were yet to come. He remembered his students at the Hardeston Institute. Watching those ignorant little minds, just thirsting for facts and new information, discover real knowledge was exciting. He missed that job.

Eric wondered just how many thousands of people had been exposed to a humanistic philosophy, together with the hard facts of science at colleges across the world. Must be millions and millions of thinkers out there. Why do people allow their governments and the big corporations to control them so, and ultimately poison their lives, and the lives of their children? Have they no backbone or do they fear the repercussions of speaking out? Or, do they think it will all naturally go away.

The public certainly needed to find truthful information and use effective solutions to cure these environmental issues. They needed a cause to get behind and millions of people needed to join that movement. Maybe it was time for him to speak-out.

Eric decided to write what he called "A letter to the people of the United States of America," and deliver it while the missions were fresh in the minds of the people.

Dear Citizens:

You don't know our names, but you've been made aware by the media of what we are doing. We are the "Eco-Terrorists" and an explanation is due.

We decided that aggressive action was necessary to make some of the big corporations aware of how they are ruining the environment and endangering the human race. Our government, and most of the governments of the world, sometimes allow bad things to happen to their citizens. Why? Greed and power. Our government and the big corporations are, in fact, partners. These powerful entities believe that the people merely exist to labor and consume for the creation of corporate profits. Those huge profits beget power. Power over the people is their ultimate goal. Power has always been achieved on the backs of the people who are lied to by their governments. It seems to be a perpetual cycle that repeats throughout history. The rich vs. the poor. The haves and the have-nots.

But today, the stakes are higher and the dangers even greater. The corporations and our negligent governments continue to play their game of power over the people, which includes their power over nature. They don't care how many people become ill or die or how many future generations will be exposed to these dangers, all because of their reckless desire for power and profits.

In the past, with great and honest intentions, many Federal agencies were set up to look after the environment and the health and safety of the people of our country. The EPA (Environmental Protection Agency), the FDA (Food and Drug Administration), the USDA (United States Department of Agriculture) all were designed for our protection.

But then greed came into play and collusion occurred.

Serious corruption has allowed these offending corporations to do what they want. Each of those agencies should monitor the corporations, levy fines and penalties. And, on the surface, they seem to do their jobs. But when it's in a corporation's interests, these government agencies look the other way. Our very important protectors have become co-conspirators.

Let me simply reduce all of this:

- *Our water is dangerously polluted.*

- *Our food is dangerously polluted.*

- *Our air is dangerously polluted.*

These are three blessings that nature has given us to stay alive: Water-Food-Air. These should all be pristine! But our necessities for life are not clean. They have become polluted and the poisons are killing us.

The government will not, or cannot stop them. That's why we've taken matters into our own hands. We, the "Eco-Terrorists," are targeting these polluters of our water, food and air. By destroying their infrastructures and operating systems and therefore their profits, we will stop these polluters.

What can you do? You can immediately send the following message to every corporation and every branch of government.

"Dear Government:

First, I support the so-called "Eco-Terrorists" and their actions.

I demand that you stop the pollution. It is not necessary to list the violators. You know who they are and what they are doing. I know you have entire departments designed to suppress the truth from the public.

I will encourage all of my friends and family to stop buying and using the goods and/or services from all known polluters. I am sending this memo to my mayor, my governor, my Congressman, my Senator and the President of the U.S.A, and to the polluting corporations.

—A Citizen of the United States of America."

Only full compliance by these serial polluters will cause us to cease our actions.

—With sincere love for humankind, the "Eco-Terrorists"

Letters and emails flooded in to corporations and government offices from all over North America. The people wanted the pollution to stop and the clean-up to begin.

In response to the complaints from the people, a statement from the government was made to the media. The release stated that Congress had passed new laws making the executives and senior staff of any violating corporation subject to severe fines and criminal sentences. Even though those kinds of statutes had long been in effect, now all Federal agencies were given instructions not to hesitate in arresting anyone guilty of disobeying the laws. The government promised a national crack-down, if only the eco-terrorists would stop their destruction.

As usual, the government had no intention of doing anything. Secretly, their actual response to this public outcry was to insist that all law enforcement agencies increase their efforts to bring this terrorism to a halt.

This, of course, was an impossible task.

Billy read the letter written by Eric.

Solemnly, he turned to Rob Collings and said. "You know these boys are becoming true folk-heroes. Only thing missing from their popularity is the revelation of their names. But, people like mystery men, you know."

Collings sensed a bit of envy in Billy's statements.

Billy continued. "The public really likes what the boys are doing. The government is shitting its pants. *Hoo-rah. Hoo-rah.* So. What's next for our little commandos, Rob?

"We've hit the Southwest, Rockies, South, Northwest, Midwest and New England. We're making government law enforcement and corporations very paranoid. The next target is a big chemical producer in New Jersey, and after that DC."

"Hmm." Billy looked out the window.

Another warning was issued to the media for general release. Billy decided to play with the details, offering more than usual. This message stated that the next target was on the West Coast.

The details appeared to be clear.

But it was a lie.

WARNING: We will attack and destroy the west coast offices and all operations of one of the companies who have been continually cited as major and habitual environmental polluters by the EPA, OSHA, FDA, USDA. You know who you are and you know what you have been doing is wrong and deadly. Now, you will be stopped.

WE ARE AMERICANS! (Not foreign terrorists) We are citizens who are fed-up with your poisoning of our environment. We will tolerate no more. We are angry. We are many. We intend to put you out of business.

NOTICE: You do not have time to locate the High Explosives planted at your facilities, nor can you know exactly where or when we will strike. No humans will be hurt from the planned destruction of your facilities if you alert them now. Moments prior to our attack we will alert your personnel to evacuate. We do not seek fatalities. However, anyone deciding to remain on your property after evacuation warnings may be subject to injury or even death.

YOU HAVE BEEN WARNED!

The infamous "Chemical Coast" of New Jersey was the next target. Nowhere in the world was there such a concentration of chemical plants. Two miles of huge toxic refineries just waiting for an accidental explosion, or leaks or spills, or an act of terrorism.

Just a stone's throw from each other were the gigantic chemical plants that processed chlorine, hydrofluoric acid, phosgene, and many other toxic chemicals, and oil and gasoline refineries and storage facilities. Railroad freight lines and commuter trains went past this array of toxin producers. Air traffic flew overhead and ships from all nations docked in the harbors. Just one major transportation accident could be disastrous. The whole area was a ticking time-bomb and anything could set it off.

Even though the EPA continued to issue citations and these corporations paid their fines, little was done to make their chemical operations safe. Many had not undergone modernization of their facilities in years.

Eric decided to target a large refinery on the coast outside of Trenton, New Jersey. One of the oldest chemical producers, they had been a continuous EPA violator. The company had always paid its fines, but the lack of proper, or more often absence of, clean-up caused the EPA to site them again and again. Not much had been done by the company to correct their methods of operation. They were using the same techniques and production operations that were used more than a hundred years ago; maybe even longer.

The refinery was located near very dense populations, so complete destruction, like the raid on the big petrochemical operation in the Texas Gulf coast, wasn't practical. Millions of people in the Pennsylvania, New Jersey and New York area could be severely affected by explosions and the resulting poisonous toxins released into the air.

Eric chose to hurt them in their pocketbooks.

The plan was to contaminate the chemical storage tanks, rendering them neutral and not usable for sale.

Billy's team crafted a message to the media for release after the mission was complete, reinforcing the idea that these domestic eco-terrorists could have caused major destruction of the chemical facilities, but chose not to put the population of the tri-state area at risk. The release would affirm that this two-mile strip of refineries on the Jersey coast remained extremely vulnerable to foreign terrorist attacks.

Chief Pangborn received an anonymous email tip. The source wasn't traceable or verifiable, but it was the first detailed lead that had come their way before one of the eco-terrorist hits. And it had an expiration date. Action had to be taken immediately. He put a call in to CIA agent Dempsey in the New York City CIA office. Dempsey was in charge of the Northeastern District.

"This might be it, Dempsey. First lead we've gotten. Looks like it's from an informer. It says: Go to 1256 Coleridge St., Unit Number 45, in Trenton, New Jersey. You'll find a crate of weapons and equipment. The terrorists will arrive about 2:00 p.m. today and you can catch them before they do more damage.—A Friend. We've just sent the copy to your office."

Dempsey was cautious. "It must be someone on the inside. Maybe one of their members has defected. Or it might just be disinformation."

Pangborn was adamant. "Doesn't matter. We've got to follow up on any lead we get, at this point. Put a team together and get out there."

Dempsey and two agents went to the address. Just as the email described, they found the huge crate in the warehouse unit. Dempsey confirmed the contents. "Looks like military stuff, alright. Close it up, boys. Take up surveillance positions outside. And I don't want any shooting unless I say so. We want them alive for interrogation."

Agent Dempsey called for a full-scale agency back up with instructions not to do anything until the alleged perpetrators had interfaced with him.

About 2:00 p.m., Clay, Eric and their team arrived at the old warehouse. Eric jumped out and opened the wooden doors to the unit. Clay backed the van inside and Eric closed the doors. Once inside, all of the team got out of the car.

Clay went over to the equipment container to retrieve the new plans. As he bent over, he noticed that the security seal was broken. Immediately, he knew they were in a trap.

Within seconds, Dempsey shouted through a bullhorn from outside: "This is the United States CIA, FBI, and NSA. Drop your weapons and come out slowly with your hands on your heads. You won't get any further warning. You are surrounded."

Clay peeked through the doors. A line of big black SUVs blocked the driveway. They were in deep trouble.

Calmly, Clay opened the containers and got out the sniper rifle and clips of ammunition, giving the gun to Ian. Clay got out the only Red HIT tube and gave it to Jake. Then he sprayed the plans and the rest of the contents with the "Gertz juice."

For a moment, Clay wished that Rob Collings had allowed them to be armed. But, no capitulation. He relished a fight.

Quickly, he ordered everybody back into the van. Ian and Jake crouched low, just below the open sunroof. Jake's Red HIT missile was repurposed as a bazooka, intended to blow a hole in the cars that blocked their escape. Ian was instructed to fire his rifle at any targets of opportunity.

Clay got behind the wheel. With tires squealing and smoking, the van broke through the wooden doors.

Jake popped through the sunroof, shoves the RED missile through and fired. A good hit. The bomb blew two of the cars blocking them apart, giving them a chance to drive through.

A hail of automatic gunfire erupted on each side of the van. Interior trim and glass flew all about.

Jake took a clean hit in the head and fell back through the sunroof. George was shot and killed instantly.

Ian managed to get off a few shots bringing down some of the agents, but the powerful gunfire increased and with half of his head blown away, Ian dropped back into the car.

Driving like a madman, Clay looked over to the passenger seat and saw that Eric had been severely shot and was bleeding profusely.

Clay tried to drive through the hole in the line of big black government vehicles, but the barrage of gunfire intensified as hundreds of bullets flew at the van.

Everywhere there were flames and explosions as the federal agents continued to fire on the burning van, maneuvering through the snaked line of black SUVs.

Clay shouted to Eric. "This is it, ol' buddy. We gave 'em hell for a while, didn't we? *Hoo-Rah! Hoo-Rah! Hoo...*"

A sniper riddled Clay with a round of bullets and he slumped over the wheel, crashing into the line of cars. The van exploded into flames.

It was over. They were all dead.

Eric Atkins and Clay Perkins, with all of their altruism and noble struggles attributed to nameless "eco-terrorists," died without notice.

Twenty

Enter: Billy

As usual, the powerful and rich, without a bit of care or concern, still controlled the lives and futures of the people. The corporations went back to their old ways and the pollution of the earth and poisoning of people continued. It was as though nothing that Eric and Clay had endured or accomplished had ever happened. All returned to as it was before their valiant efforts.

It remained for another man, on another day, to correct the corruption and tribulations that beset mankind.

Somewhere on the Gulf Coast, hidden deep in the WFJ Corporation headquarters, Billy Johnstone was quietly talking with his aide, Rob Collings.

A beep tone from Billy's computer interrupted them. Billy opened the email, perused the message and then read it aloud. "Listen to this, Rob. 'At 3:00 p.m. today, the CIA, FBI, and NSA, in a joint operation, intercepted the eco-terrorist group involved in the destruction of oil refineries, electric generation plants and many more acts of violence. All of the terrorists were killed in a raid at Trenton, New Jersey. No other group or organization has taken credit for these acts of violence. Presently, it is not known who the terrorists were and whether this group operated alone or was part of a larger organization.'"

Billy, oddly calm, looked at Rob. "Damn. Eric and Clay are dead. Gunned down by the Feds. And they were the good guys; so sincere... They really believed that they could make a difference. Well, by God, they almost did!"

Collings was stunned. "I thought we were bullet-proof. We were so careful. How the hell did the Feds find them?"

Billy was firm. "Mistakes happen. But, Rob, I'd like you to look into it, if you will. If we discover that this was more than just a mistake... Well, I wouldn't want to be that guy when we find him."

Billy got up energetically and fixed himself a drink. "What a sad day. Gonna miss those two guys. But, you know Rob, I warned them of the possibility of failure. I told them it was very doubtful, even if they were successful, that any of their work would have a lasting impact on the corporate and government greed. Unfortunately, Rob, life will go on as usual. With or without Eric Atkins or Clay Perkins."

Billy took a long, satisfying pull from his drink. "See, you can't fight city hall. Oh, you can fight 'em, I suppose. But you can't win. Those government folks have all the power and resources. And they never forget. The only way to wage war on the government and their laws is to become the government and enact your own laws. If you're in charge, then you're the winner!"

On the surface, Billy's pragmatic speech seemed to be unfeeling. But Rob believed that Billy was genuinely hurt, and very angry at what had happened.

Billy used the desktop communications panel to signal an emergency meeting with his Inner Circle advisors.

In a short time, they were all assembled in the meeting room. Billy stood at the head of the conference table and turned to his loyal supporters. He spoke calmly, sincerely. "Eric Atkins and Clay Perkins are dead. They were murdered by our neo-conservative, self-centered, corrupt, fascist government. In the end, none of them give a damn about what Eric and Clay were fighting for. Our government is totally committed to some kind of last-man-standing game. They're stuck in that so-called Darwinian theory of 'survival of the fittest.'"

Billy started pacing and his speech became more animated. "In fact, what they're doing is walking us all down a slow and inhumane road to extinction. It could take hundreds of years to weed out those that are the fittest, leaving the ones that they want to survive and become the powerful. In the meantime, the breeding of more and more people takes place adding to the numbers of people that can't or won't keep up with the changes in technology. By disregarding rampant population growth, the government completely overlooks the resulting social issues that prevent their misguided plan from coming to fruition. They don't really care about pollution, or the people. They don't realize that in their negligence and their half-baked concepts of totalitarianism they are likely to wipe out all of mankind."

Billy was on a roll, now. "Oh, I understand the reasoning behind their game. They want to maintain their power over the people. For a long time they've used social thought control to manage the natural instincts of mankind. Been using movies, TV, video games, and and now the internet to influence not only the kids, but the adults as well, showing them violence as an amusement, under the guise of entertainment. Kid shows teaching the young how to be dishonest and delivered as innocent fun. They've desensitized several generations into thinking that lying, cheating, maiming and killing are the normal ways of living."

Billy's speech soared to a feverish pitch. "Our government officials are corrupt and they've become immoral models that state and local government officials and the citizens themselves follow. And they're teaching the young that their arbitrary rules and regulations must be blindly obeyed, or you're automatically a traitor! Everything about society is so mired in politics and greed that honesty and integrity are no more. 'Things' matter more than people. If you've got money, anything goes. Materialism versus humanity never ends well. This kind of immorality is very dangerous. I fear we're headed for a disastrous end."

Billy took a deep breath and stood up straight, speaking calmly once again. "Their version, their system of governance is the problem. See, governments can't continue to operate the way they do. These systems are outdated. They just create bigger and bigger messes, faster and faster. But be assured, gentlemen, all of those messes can be straightened out, and in short order, too. I've got a plan to correct these problems."

The men hung on every word. They were absolutely mesmerized. Billy was a skillful and convincing actor.

Rob Collings knew how really well this man could perform.

Billy paused for a moment and spoke to his followers once more quietly and sincerely, in an almost prayer-like fashion. "May God bless Eric Atkins and Clay Perkins. Eric was right, you know. He was sincere about stopping pollution and saving our environment. Both of them gave their lives for what they believed in. I really liked both of those boys."

As a skilled orator might do, Billy changed his tone. "But they are gone now. They're dead. May they rest in peace. *Semper Fi*! We will carry on the battle for those good men. And someday soon, I will erect a monument to them."

With that somewhat disingenuous last remark from Billy, Rob Collings knew that something was not right. He could always tell.

But Billy Johnstone was on one of his legendary tirades. "Listen up, people. For every problem, there is an answer. But first, you have to find the cause of the problem. You have to know how you got to where you are. In this instance, the cause is man himself, who in his greed and zeal, has considered nature as his own renewable resource. That's the first mistake. It's just ain't true. The earth doesn't really care. Nature will repair itself. Ol' Mother Nature has all the time she wants. But mankind doesn't have that kind of time. Man will continue to ask of nature until nature will take no more. She'll stop puttin' out for man, and then we'll all die. My God, those in charge today are dead wrong. As a result of their stupidity, we're killing ourselves. Sure, sure we've made great technical advances, but at what cost to mankind? Oh, it's a hell of a mess, boys."

Billy was wound up again. "Listen, there are a lot of bright men and women looking at every part of our present technological nightmare and they've found better and cleaner ways. I want to work with those guys. They're worth having on my team. The government of this country and the rulers of the other nations of the world won't listen to these fresh-thinking people. Their new ideas might disrupt some old money-making system, or cost a lot to retrofit. Now, the prevailing systems are based on money, and the money guys don't give a damn about the environment or the people. They just love the power they have over everything."

Rob was preoccupied. He mumbled. "Poor Eric and Clay saw the truth. That's what killed them." Rob was quite certain that someone had tipped off the CIA about Eric and Clay's last raid. There was no doubt for him that it was a set-up. A deliberate ambush...

Billy switched gears again. "In the meantime, the human herd keeps on producing more and more people. So, whatcha gonna do with all those millions of new people and those who didn't make the cut? The ones who didn't make it through the government-mandated 'teach to the test' dumbed-down education system we're stuck with now? I went out to several of our own factories and found this 'gotta get it right and obey the rules' system was being used. I was stymied for a while. But, it got me thinking about the whole deal. And then, I came up with an idea. It's a plan to quickly, and finally, change the flawed systems of government and corporations. Really reward the skilled and responsible worker and at the same time deal with those who are not able, or don't want to help society."

Billy stopped for a moment. "Are you with me, boys? This world is filled up with clutter and chaos. Governments and organizations and technologies that aren't functional or necessary. Most only care about themselves. The people, long ago, should have rebelled against all of this crap and corruption. Why didn't they revolt? Fear! They've always been controlled by the rich. Well, I'll give them their overdue rebellion and none of those rich bastards will live through it, and that's a promise!"

Billy looked at Rob, ensuring he, too, was paying attention. Then he spoke deliberately. "See, the scum are the polluters…the schemers, the criminals, the loafers, the opportunists, the capitalists, the lawyers, the bankers and a lot of people that can't or won't work. Well, all of that needs to be done away with. Mankind has been around too long not to have learned the lessons that have kept him on this merry-go-round. Listen, I'm gonna change the entire system of doing things and clean up this country and every nation in the world. When I do, those old notions of corruption, poverty, crime, sickness and pollution will be out the window. I'll send all of those misfits to Hell where they belong!"

Billy's passion rose. "We've got the technology and I've got the ideas, and you boys know it. I really understand what to do. Put me in that White House and I'll give the world and it's people the cleaning and scrubbing they've needed since the beginning of time."

Billy had them captivated. Every man was attentive.

Billy wound up his speech, slowing down a bit. "Why boys, it'll be as easy as *A-B-C*. *A*, we get elected. *B*, we change the system and eliminate everything and everyone that doesn't work. And, *C*, we control it all and make sure it doesn't backslide. It won't be a good time to be a bystander. I need people who will work. I'll remake this world into the beautiful utopia that God meant it to be, with no war, or strife and plenty for all. Now's the time to act, boys. Let's make it happen!"

The men applauded approvingly.

With his usual abruptness, Billy interrupted their enthusiasm. "Thank you all. Gentlemen, this meeting's over."

Rob Collings had a momentary flash of intuition. Did Eric and Clay get too close to becoming real heroes? Even though the world didn't know their names, they had been making headlines, especially after Eric's letter. No one had ever upstaged Billy. He wouldn't let it happen. Was Billy the snitch?

After all of the men had departed, Rob turned to Billy. "Okay, they all bought what you said, and for the most part, I do too. They'll get behind you Billy, and follow you wherever you want to go. To the man, they're loyal to you. But now, my commander in chief, tell ol' Rob the truth. Did you set up Eric and Clay to be ambushed?"

Billy was startled at the question and stammered a little when he answered. "No-no, no I didn't, Rob." Regaining his composure after a moment he added. "I didn't rat them out. And, if I had, so what? They're dead. I warned them that this might happen. Their plans might have worked, someday. Truthfully, I thought what they were doing was like a piss in the Pacific Ocean; it wouldn't be noticed or make a difference, and they might get killed in the process. Well, they took their chances and they got killed."

Recapturing his former confidence and enthusiasm Billy walked around the room talking maniacally to the air. "But, no more chances! We'll do it my way, now. Oh, I've got ideas, I really do, Rob. It's gonna be my turn at bat, and with ol' Billy at the plate, we'll win every game. We'll be the winners."

Suddenly Billy turned and directed his statements at Collings. "Robbie, when I become president, I'm gonna change the world. And believe me, my plans will work! The people will love their new way of living. They're gonna be happy, happy, happy…"

Rob stood expressionless, staring back at Billy.

"Listen, Rob. Don't you worry. Making these changes will be easy as *A-B-C*. In the end, you can rest assured that everything's gonna be all right…and that's a promise!"

Water good.

Man hurt water.

Water dead.

Man dead.

—SO SAID THE DOLPHIN

...This is the way the world ends
This is the way the world ends
This is the way the world ends
Not with a bang but a whimper.

—T.S. Eliot

.

Acknowledgements

I sincerely thank my treasured daughter, Jane, not least for providing the title for this first book. Without her commitment to make literate sense of my manuscripts and her diligence in copyediting and proofing, none of the three books in this series would be possible.

ABOUT THE AUTHOR

STEVEN J. CONNERS was born in Dayton, Ohio. After nearly four decades in the entertainment industry, Conners "retired" to host a radio show, *The Voice of Reason*, in order to provide a platform for everyone's voice to be heard. His years of traveling the country and speaking with "the average person" inspired his recent fiction efforts, *The Madness of Power* series.

Conners worked in live theatre, creating, directing and producing numerous stage productions that traveled the United States, including *The Great Ghost Show* and *The Magic Land of Mother Goose*, before moving into the management and creation of event-style stunt promotions. In between tours and booking *Dilly the Dragon, The Six-Foot Chocolate Easter Bunny, The Magic Elf, Silkini's Frozen Alive* and *Silkini's Buried Alive*, Conners made a foray into designing and setting up several restaurants and even had a go at running a catering business (Shindigs Unlimited) and his own jazz club (Bozo's).

In addition to *The Madness of Power* series, Conners has written plays, children's books, a biography of showman Jack Baker, and a non-fiction book on the responsibilities of democratic liberty.

He continues to travel and maintains a home base in Reno, Nevada.